Stories
from
the Tube

Stories
from
the Tube

Matthew Sharpe

Villard ❧ New York

All rights reserved under International and Pan-American Copyright Conventions. Published in the United States by Villard Books, a division of Random House, Inc., New York, and simultaneously in Canada by Random House of Canada Limited, Toronto.

VILLARD BOOKS is a registered trademark of Random House, Inc.

Some of these stories were originally published, in slightly different form, in *American Letters & Commentary, Harper's, Mississippi Mud, Southwest Review,* and *Zoetrope.*

Library of Congress Cataloging-in-Publication Data

Sharpe, Matthew.
Stories from the tube / Matthew Sharpe.
p.   cm.
Contents: Tide—Cloud—In the snowy kingdom—The woman who—
Rose in the house—A car—How I greet my daughter—Bridesmaids—
Doctor Mom—A bird accident.
ISBN 0-375-50196-7
1. United States—Social life and customs—20th century—Fiction.
2. Television advertising—Adaptations.   3. Family—United States—
Fiction.   I. Title.
PS3569.H3444S7   1998
813'.54—dc21   98-20057

Random House website address: www.randomhouse.com
Printed in the United States of America on acid-free paper
24689753
First Edition
DESIGN BY MERCEDES EVERETT

Hey Susanna,
it's a family buy!

"The revolution will not be televised."

—Gil Scott-Heron,
as quoted in a TV advertisement for sneakers

Contents

Stories
from
the Tube

Tide

A mother and her small daughter open the trunk
of the car to find the daughter's leotard has
a red, wet stain on it.

DAUGHTER: And the ballet's tomorrow!
MOTHER: Honey, we'll get it out.
MOTHER, VOICE-OVER: . . . So I crossed my fingers
and threw it in.

—TV advertisement for laundry detergent

DON'T DO THAT" AND "I LOVE YOU"—WHO KNOWS WHICH words I use more with my daughter, Jenny? Whenever I come home from work she's in the midst of some wild action. She gathers all the neighborhood boys around her, and they rig bike-jumping ramps out of scrap wood and bricks in my driveway. She rushes up one ramp on her mountain bike, sails through the air like that motorcycle daredevil who they say has broken every bone in his body at least twice, and slams down onto another ramp six feet away. The boys do it too, but she is their leader. In between the two ramps they put things you wouldn't really want to put in there. One of the boys will volunteer his pet gerbil, say. Or if they can, get a small dog to sit in there. Jenny herself has these rodent-size friends that she makes out of dust, but they're very important to her and she won't endanger them, especially after what happened a while ago. Lacking an animal, they'll put a doll in, or they'll save up the jagged lids off cans of dog food.

Once at the end of a long day at the hospital I approached the house in my car just as Jenny came raging into the street on her bike after a jump, completely out of control. I got right out of my car and screamed at all of them, they could be crushed in an instant, didn't that mean anything to them, et cetera. I forbade Jenny to use her bike for a week, and I confiscated their ramp materials. That's why it was such a shock when they did it again last week. I bet I know what happened: Jenny cajoled all the boys to hunt down new materials and build a new ramp in my driveway. They did it for Jenny because she has a power over them. It makes me think of the rock-and-roll song by that foursome of ugly boys in black leather that Jenny watches on TV: "But she ain't no tomboy when she puts her tongue in my mouth."

As for the dust, I say, "don't play with that. what's so great about dust?" She doesn't listen. I let her slide on the little things. I'm telling you, she's fierce. Never had a father, I'm sure that's it.

Recently, just before the bicycle incident, I had a nice loaf of white bread. When I got home from work she was sawing off all the crust with a big serrated knife. She's nine years old. "Look, Mom, I'm skinning it."

"This is what you do when I'm not around?"

There was a pot of oil over a high flame on the stove. She dropped in the naked white bread. "I'm boiling it in oil."

"Jenny. Jenny," I said. It's strange to say her name out loud because it's my name too. She pulled it out with tongs. "Grew a new skin," she said. "Let's try it on Saint Francis." He was one of her dust pals. She took him out of his cage and threw him right into the pot. Then she ran around the kitchen, beside herself. "He's screaming! He's screaming!" She ran up to the pot, and I think she would have thrust her hand in to save him if I hadn't caught her arm. There wasn't much left of him afterward.

Next day by the time I got home she had another pot of oil on and she had caught a mouse in a Hav-a-Hart trap. As I entered the kitchen she lifted the mouse out of the trap by its tail with her thumb and forefinger and dangled it over the pot of boiling oil.

I said, "You wouldn't dare." I shouldn't have said that.

You should see the way she dances. she's in a ballet/ modern class. She leaps wildly and tumbles hard. She was up on pointe in a week. She throws her little body around as if it were a rag doll. She's really driven. She works herself to death, practically.

This year her class is putting on Stravinsky's *Rite of Spring.* I came home one day and she said, "I got the part of the Virgin!" I couldn't remember the ballet well. I thought I must have seen it once because I had the distinct impression there was no Virgin in there. But I was happy for Jenny. I made her favorite dinner that night, pasta puttanesca. It worries me the way she dances, as if she has nothing to lose.

And the things she thinks about worry me. After dinner that night—this is about a month ago—she asked me, "When am I gonna start to bleed?"

"What?"

"Bleed. When am I gonna bleed?"

"Oh. I didn't know what the hell you were talking about. That's sort of inaccurate, to call your period bleeding."

"All right, so when am I gonna get my period?"

"What's the hurry?"

"Because then I'll be a woman."

"No you won't."

"Yes."

"Think of thirteen-year-olds you know. Are they women?"

"Maybe."

"Listen. Womanhood is more than just physical. It's emotional too. It has to do with experience."

"But doesn't your body teach you something? When you have your first period, don't you automatically know something that you didn't know before?"

"No."

"Mo-o-om." Her face was all red. I think I was scaring her. What is it that I say that I keep scaring her?

"It's true," I said, "that womanhood cannot begin until you ovulate. But actual womanhood per se comes later. It's the consequence of your desires."

"What's the consequence of your desires?"

"It varies. Mostly weariness, I think."

"No, what's the consequence of *your* desires?"

"Oh." Now I understood. "You, sweetie."

"What was that one word you used a second ago? 'Obligate' or something?"

"Ovulate."

"Lisa and Tina just talked about bleeding. What's 'ovulate'?"

"You mean all you know about menstruation is what you heard from two other fourth-graders?"

"What's menstruation?"

"Oh boy." I do happen to be a registered nurse, and you'd think that would have given me some handle on how to tell my daughter about this. Not so. " 'Menstruation,' " I said, "comes from the Latin '*mensis*,' meaning month, because you menstruate once a month, more or less. 'Ovulate' is from the Latin '*ovum*,' meaning egg. It's the production of the egg and its journey from the ovary through the fallopian tubes to the uterus."

"I'm lost."

I cleared the dishes and took the pad of paper and the pencil down from near the phone. Sitting at the kitchen table, I drew her one of those as-seen-from-the-front pictures of the vagina, the cervix, the uterus, the fallopian tubes, and the ovaries that looks like a ram's head with a gas mask on. I know this stuff like I know the back of my hand, but my heart was pounding. How do you explain this to your nine-year-old daughter? I just reached into my head and pulled out whatever was there.

"Okay, a girl is born with all these follicles, maybe two, three million follicles *here*," I said, pointing with my pencil. "Every month or so, some of the follicles grow eggs."

"Eggs? No way."

"Not like sunny-side up. Much smaller. No shell. The eggs are very delicate. The whole reproductive apparatus is like a glass statue."

"But I thought everything in there is all soft and mushy."

"Very soft."

"So how can it be like a glass statue? Is it clear, like see-through?"

"No."

"How do you know? Maybe it is see-through."

"I promise you it's not."

"What about the glass statue?"

"Forget about the glass statue. I made a mistake."

"Maybe you're making a mistake now. How am I supposed to know which one is the mistake?"

"Jenny. The menstrual cycle is complicated. Why don't you let me get all the way through my explanation and then come at me with your usual questions and challenges to my authority?"

She answered by sighing like an actress and letting her head drop sideways onto the kitchen table just a little faster and harder than is comfortable for a mother to watch. Her face was looming above the diagram now, and she peered down at it with one eye.

At this point I was like one of those soldiers from rural Ohio or wherever who has been wounded in battle and, as he's drifting off to death, begins to recite long biblical passages in fluent Aramaic, only instead of the Bible it was the nursing-school textbook I was recalling verbatim. "As the follicles grow the egg, they also produce a hormone called estrogen. Estrogen causes the endometrium, which is the uterine lining— here—to grow and thicken. Then the follicle releases the egg into the fallopian tube, ruptures, and produces progesterone, which causes the endometrium to make food for an embryo. The embryo is like the teeny tiny baby that happens if a sperm swims through all that mucus and nails the egg."

"Is that where the blood comes from? The sperm nailing the egg?"

Have I somehow insidiously passed on to Jenny her penchant for the macabre? It's possible. The last thing I tried to explain to her that night was the sloughing off of the ovum in the vaginal secretions. She pounced. "What's that word, 'sluff'?"

"Every book I've ever seen on the female reproductive cycle uses that word. Can't you figure it out from the context?"

"Can't you just tell me what it means?"

I went to the dictionary on top of the piano in the den. She didn't follow me in there, so I had to lug the thing back into the kitchen. It just so happens that I was having my own monthly cramps at that time. I opened the dictionary feeling tired and annoyed, and in my haste I made a mistake. " 'Slough. One. A marshy, muddy place or swamp. Two. A state of hopeless dejection.' "

———

THE FOLLOWING NIGHT AT DINNER JENNY SAID, "SO, MOM, LISA and Tina and me came back early from recess and I took them into the coat closet and told them all that stuff about sluffing and endometrium and obligation. They didn't get it. I don't get it either. What does any of it have to do with getting your period?"

"That's it. That's the period."

"What's the period?"

"Endometrium and obligation."

"But what does it mean?"

"Maybe you were right yesterday when you said your body will teach you something when you have your period. Before that I can say 'prostoglandin estrogen progesterone' until I'm blue in the face, but you'll still be in the dark."

"Come on, Mom, can't you just explain it to me?"

"No."

"Bullshit."

"Jenny!"

I wanted to cry when she said that to me. She had a furious frown on her small face. I figured I could either fight her about the language and watch her explode before my eyes, or I could try to help her on her quest. I saw she was in pain from not knowing. But is knowledge going to make her any less of a willful little beast? I don't think so.

"All right," I said. "There's an old folktale about a mom and a daughter. The daughter is sick. She's in bed. She's got a headache, cramps, maybe a nosebleed, I don't know what." Jenny's frown slackened a bit—that's a big relief for a mother. "Her mom is trying to take care of her," I said, "but she doesn't really know what's wrong. Finally the daughter says, 'There's something in the garden that will cure me.' The mom says, 'Is it the potato?' and the daughter says, 'Mom, you're so stupid. It's not the potato.' So the mom says, 'Is it the cucumber?' and the daughter says, 'Well, you're getting warm, but you're still fairly much of a foolish, insipid mother. It's not the cucumber.' And then the mom says, 'Uh, could it be, I don't know, say, the gardener?' 'Bingo!' End of story."

We sat in silence for a moment at the kitchen table. Jenny knitted her brow, put her chin in her hands, pursed her lips. Then she spoke: "When the mom said, 'cucumber,' why did the daughter say, 'You're getting warm'?"

MAYBE I DIDN'T EMPHASIZE ENOUGH HOW DISTRESSING THIS business of careening out into the street on the bicycle is. The second time it happened, a week and a half ago, I had to brake hard in order not to hit her. I even banged my head on the steering wheel. For a moment I sat in the car stunned while Jenny stood inches from the front fender straddling her bike. Then I got out of the car and slammed the door, and I was so furious I cried. "Get away!" I shouted at the two little ruffians on their bikes in my driveway. I'm sure they were relieved not to have to stick around and watch Jenny's mother crying.

I told Jenny to just go inside while I unloaded the trunk of the car. I had been to the supermarket, and I had been to the store to pick up Jenny's white Virgin costume for the dance. Instead of going in, Jenny followed the car into the driveway on her bicycle and stood next to the car door when

I opened it and followed me around to the trunk. When I opened the trunk, the first thing we saw was Jenny's white leotard with a big, wet, dark red stain on it. The grape-juice bottle must have exploded when I braked for her. "God, it looks as if you've been bleeding," I said without thinking.

"Like having my period?"

That night I told her this behavior simply had to stop, and to make sure that it did, she would not be allowed to dance in the dance this year. When she heard that, she went to the kitchen wall and started to pull pots and pans and big serving spoons off their hooks and throw them across the room, shouting and screaming. I had to run over and restrain her before she threw something that would shatter and blind one of us. I came up behind her and grabbed her wrists. I felt her strong little muscles, I felt all her power moving against me. Finally, in order to calm her down I had to just hug her with all my might.

———————

THE DANCE WAS A WEEK AFTER THE GRAPE-JUICE EXPLOSION. Jenny behaved almost as if nothing had happened, only she was more subdued than her usual self, which is to say she was not herself at all. That made me feel terrible. I called up the head of her ballet school and made a deal with her. She and I would pretend that Jenny was out of the dance, but she'd have Jenny continue to rehearse the part of the Virgin as an understudy, "just in case." At the last minute, I'd tell Jenny I changed my mind. I can't remember if that was my original intention when I forbade her to dance. I really was upset about the collision—I mean the near-collision—but Jenny lives for dancing, and if a mother is intentionally hurtful to her daughter, then she is a bad mother.

I went to the store and bought some of that detergent with bleach that I'd seen advertised on TV. I did the presoak, washed it, soaked again, washed, and the stain was gone. Not that I loved the idea of her prancing around onstage in that particular costume anyway. It was so tight you could see everything when she had it on—her protruding pelvic bones, her ribs, everything.

When I broke the news to her that she was back in the dance, she did not appear surprised. She smiled calmly, like someone who knows something you don't know.

———

THE PARENTS IN THE AUDIENCE GASPED WHEN, TEN MINUTES INTO the dance, the fierce, pale Virgin leapt onto the stage from the wings. She had taken something—red lipstick? red nail polish?—and smeared it on the front of her leotard, mostly around the crotch and the breasts (she doesn't really have breasts yet—around the tender little buds of her nipples). I knew instantly that this was Jenny's own doing. This was vintage Jenny. And now it all came together, now I understood. I was terribly proud. What a costume!

After the ballet I went backstage. All the girls were squealing and hugging each other. The head of the ballet school, a dignified woman in her fifties, was wandering among the girls, patting this one and that one on the head. I saw her approach Jenny, look at her with an expression of puzzlement that I recognized from the inside out, and walk away. I saw Jenny watch her walk away: she looked after her wistfully, and then she looked down at the floor. I realized that not even Jenny could have done what she did that night without also feeling the shame.

I called out to my daughter. She looked up, ran to me, hugged my waist, and said, uncertainly, "I killed tonight, didn't I, Mom?"

"Yes, sweetheart," I said. "You killed."

Cloud

A woman is sitting on an airplane when she is approached by a cloud:

CLOUD: Excuse me, uh, I'm in the window seat.
WOMAN: Vacation?
CLOUD: No, no, convention in Anaheim. I'm one of the clouds who makes White Cloud, the softer, thicker bathroom tissue? I'm boring you.

—TV advertisement for toilet paper

IT WAS ALREADY LATE WHEN THE TOPIC CAME UP. THE SIX OF them were sitting around Barbara Sternberg's living room still doggedly sipping the Merlot. Barbara had made her five friends steak, plain and simple. Someone had brought a three-bean salad, and someone had brought a chanterelle-mushroom thing. All of the food had been devoured, along with many bottles of wine, and it was really quite late. One of Barbara's friends asked, without knowing what can of worms she was opening, "Hey, whatever happened to Lisa Cornerson? She worked in various production departments. Remember her? She was a wild thing. If you wanted to know where the party was, you looked for Lisa Cornerson."

Other people said:

"Yeah, Lisa Cornerson."

"She was a few years older than us."

"She was nice, but she always seemed sad to me."

"Can somebody please explain to me the appeal of a career in magazine production?"

"She disappeared. Lisa Cornerson."

Wasn't Barbara always the host of the more or less annual get-together of the original six? Fresh from college, they had been thrown together as editorial assistants. In the last dozen years, each had made a good-to-brilliant series of moves within the New York magazine business, working the circuit from Hearst to Condé Nast to Hachette to Gruner & Jahr to Wenner to Time-Warner to *The New York Times* and back to Condé Nast. It seemed, even to themselves at times, like a wonderful life, but without ever having to say it, they all agreed on what the compromise was; it was not the sum of small, daily compromises of the industry, like cutting a seven-thousand-word essay on the ideological underpinnings of the American penal system down to a five-hundred-word sidebar on women who kill their husbands, but the Compromise, the hunkering down in one small kingdom, the vast uncharted possibilities purposefully cut away, that wild life of the body and mind they relinquished forever the instant they had picked up the crowns and placed them upon their own heads.

At the mention of Lisa Cornerson, Barbara remained quiet. It really was she who put on these evenings more often than anyone else, because they all, including Barbara, felt she somehow owed it to them. She was having the most radiant career: executive editor of *the* hard-news/celebrity magazine, consultant to several industry leaders, and, lately, the occasional appearance on television. She remained quiet and they looked at her. She was beautiful. Without trying, she had elegant posture that supported her wild, dark blond hair, tonight neatly pulled back. She was also a little worn out, or at least worn down, despite her amazing energy for both work and recreation; her amazing energy, even, for relaxation.

"You knew Cornerson quite well," Malcolm Browning said to her. There was a policy of challenging Barbara, an irreverence within a framework of admiration. You challenged her to learn from how she responded. Except Malcolm, the maverick, whose challenges were genuine and heartfelt. He had jumped the editorial tracks and surrounded himself with software. He was now fully in software, consulting for magazine groups and contributing, once in a blue moon, an article on electronic communities or what have you. He married straight out of college, years before the other two married members of the group (Barbara was not one). In the group's division of labor, Malcolm's responsibility was to imply Barbara's life choices were trivial, from the perspective of a family man.

"Lisa Cornerson was my best friend for several years," Barbara said. Her statement was surrounded by silence. Something momentous was happening within Barbara—they could see it on her face. That was why she was who she was.

"So what happened to her?" said Rick Stein.

"She disappeared," reiterated Linda Lazar, one of the married women.

"Yes," Barbara said, "Lisa Cornerson is a person about whom people say, 'She disappeared.' In fact I happen to know she made a phone call at the precise moment of her disappearance. Not everyone makes the phone call, but Lisa did. I happen to know she lives in Maine, does production on an agricultural trade magazine, is married. I can't help thinking it was one of those marriages to the first semistable, semidecent guy who came along, an SOS marriage," she said, looking at Malcolm. "I've fallen completely out of touch with her."

"You're holding back, Sternberg."

"Nope."

"You know something juicy."

"Not that I'm going to tell any of you."

"Yes you are."

"Oh, for Christ's sake. It would be completely pathetic of me to believe you won't all drop this one into the gossip mill at your earliest convenience, but let's try to maintain as much decency as you could fit on the head of a pin. So nobody interrupts me, and nobody laughs, because this is not a funny story. This is, in fact, a very strange story."

"I might interrupt," Malcolm said.

"Shut up, Malcolm," a few people said.

Barbara uncorked a fresh bottle of Merlot, filled each glass, settled back into her favorite chair, and arranged herself in a position comfortable enough to tell what she had to tell, though really it was late. "Lisa Cornerson was, as we know, a creature of the night. She always stayed out drinking, usually screwed some guy, ran back to that provisional little apartment for a couple hours of sleep, showed up at work twenty minutes late and hungover. She had been living that life for four years by the time we were getting our first jobs out of college. She let me tag along with her every night. I lived the Lisa Cornerson life, because I was already who I was and I was trying to be somebody else, too.

"Lisa understood me and I understood her, or so we thought. I saw her every night for three years. Then something happened. There began to be this feeling of someone who didn't enjoy her enjoyment, who carried her wild drinking life and her wild sex life forward from night to night, improvising the identical distraction over and over."

"She wasn't ambitious enough for you," Malcolm said.

"I think what you mean is, she wasn't ambitious enough for *you*," Barbara said. "After she and I stopped being friends, her mother died. Her father was already dead. Everybody in this room has both parents, except me. And I complain about my father—how distant he is, how sexist, how stupid, how inept at his own emotions—but my dad is also this anchor for me, as all your parents are for you. Lisa didn't have that. She was an orphan, alone in the world.

"When her mother died, Lisa changed her life. She stopped going out. She moved up to the house in Mount Vernon where her mother had lived for the last six years. She didn't sleep around anymore. Barring one tedious indiscretion in the bathroom of a Halloween party with a guy wearing a Batman cowl, she didn't have sex for a year and a half. And the Batman thing just proved she was still willing to believe in the comfort of a reckless action.

"She was now print manager for that health-and-fitness magazine. When she told me all of this quite a few years later, she said she had liked being weighed down by the job. 'I was happy being a production nimnoe,' she said. On weekends she had house-fixing projects, and in the spring she planted tomatoes, string beans, cucumbers, snow peas, and a few kinds of herbs in the backyard of her dead mother's house."

"Gee, that's cheery," said a freelance writer named Beth Falco, who was the other unmarried woman in the group.

"Yes, it was sad. Even she said she was digging in to her small life."

"When did she admit this to you? I thought you said you and she weren't friends anymore."

"Maybe nine years later, I ran into her on Forty-third and Madison, and that marked the official ending of her disappearance. She invited me to dinner up in Mount Vernon, 'because I have something to tell you,' she said. She had picked me out as the person to tell her story to. Some people, after they disappear, come back, and if they're back it means something went bad in the disappearance, and so it's very good to be back, and good to tell someone about having been gone, especially someone who has never been gone, and never will go, which is me."

"But Lisa Cornerson is gone again," said Beth, sounding worried or upset.

"Yes. Lisa tried to come back but didn't quite make it back. She never completely rematerialized."

"Come on, get to the story," said Rick Stein, a jovial senior editor with long hair, whom everyone knew Beth Falco had a longtime crush on.

"All right. It begins on an airplane. Every other Friday evening Lisa Cornerson flew to Iowa City to be on press Saturday with her magazine. Can we all picture her? The dark brown curly hair? The blue eyes? The hunched-over posture? The reddish skin that sort of glowed? Why am I talking about her in the past tense? She lives up in Maine, married to some guy."

"Married! You call that living?" Malcolm said, though whether he was commenting on the state of his own marriage or on Barbara's presumed attitude toward wedlock it was hard to say.

"The airplane hadn't yet left the ground. She always took the window seat. Someone's briefcase spilled into her lap. She didn't know what was in her lap—it should have been papers, but it was soft. Whatever it was, she shoved it off her lap and someone gathered it up into the briefcase from which it had spilled. She didn't look up to see whose brief-case. But something had already transpired between her and this man; she knew it was a man. She turned her whole body toward the window, but already some of him had rubbed off on her, was how she put it.

"As the plane was taking off she turned and peripherally took in his suit, a pale brown cashmere. Again there was this unexpected softness of the suit, the suit not entirely solid and formed, something with wavy borders. He swung in a little closer to her, and his movements had the same half-formed quality as the suit. He wasn't moving so much as growing toward her, or re-creating himself in slivers of space that were closer and closer to her body. 'Sorry about the briefcase,' he said.

"The plane was accelerating up into the air, which always frightened her. She didn't feel like being bothered, and she turned away from the man. Apart from the sheer *weirdness* of him, she considered his whole approach thus far banal. But she was laughing—a rush of giggles at just the wrong time. 'Did I say something funny?' he asked. She waved his question away without turning to look at him. 'Sorry about the briefcase,' he said again, which made her laugh even harder. Now she turned to him in the full stupidity of her laughing fit. A shock of grayish blond hair had fallen into his face. He looked arrogant. Then he looked pained and innocent, like an earnest teenager.

"There must have been something in her face that said it was okay to strike up a conversation. He prattled for a while. She was too distracted to know what he was saying—the plane surging upward and the guy somehow hovering in his seat, not making contact with the seat, it seemed, expanding and contracting.

"The collar of her blouse had rolled up in the back. He reached over and adjusted it. The joint of his thumb was icy on the nape of her neck. She said, 'What are you doing?' loudly, and several people turned around in their seats to look at her. The man retracted his hand and jerked his head away from her, his motions continuing to have a seasick quality. He looked shocked, and she felt it was she who had done something inappropriate. 'What I meant was, what are you doing? As in, what do you do?' He said he was a salesman, off and on, for National Color Press, which is the press where Lisa did her press okays. Every other week he came to New York to meet with clients, and he always took the same flight back. 'I don't know how long this job will last,' he said. 'It is in my nature to be and not to be.' This was one of the things men say that are either poetic or creepy. He took a piece of paper and a pen out of his briefcase, wrote something, and handed her the paper. It said, 'I want to learn to touch you in a way that will not be upsetting for you.'

" 'Isn't it possible to meet the man you're going to marry and know right away it's him?' Lisa thought. She handed the paper back to him, turned her body toward the window, and pressed the heels of her palms into her eyeballs. She saw the same thing she always saw when she did this: a checkerboard, spinning around; the center of the checkerboard was a whirlpool; all of the black and white squares were spinning downward into the vortex; there were always fresh new squares at the edges of the checkerboard, but then these too fell down into the deep, invisible center of the whirlpool. 'I'm married,' she said, and he said, 'This wouldn't interfere with that, I promise.' They were high above the clouds now. She looked down at the clouds, and they appeared as one surface, rigid and continuous.

"After a period of silence he left his seat. He didn't come back until the plane had landed, and then only to collect his briefcase. He smiled at her quickly and seemed embarrassed. As he walked away she thought the extent to which she was attracted to him was the extent to which she was not a healthy person, and the extent to which she deserved him was the extent to which she was not a good person.

"There were two weeks until she would be taking that flight again. For the first week she threw herself into a schedule of socializing. She returned to bars and apartments that had once been familiar. She drank as much as she could, but it wasn't working. She felt herself apart from the natural, committed drinkers. She sat still and watched them and their talk swirl around her. Once she had been in the swirl. She wondered if there had been someone back then watching her as she now watched these other people, wondering what the big fuss was about.

"In the second week after the flight, she stayed home every night and did not feel alone. She felt spied on, or lightly touched. "This must be self-awareness," she thought. It was a discomfort she was eager to spend time with. One night after work she was standing at her kitchen sink washing a leaf of red cabbage for a salad and she felt someone touching her right here, where the back of the arm meets the upper back. The hand slid gently down her side and came to rest on her hip. This was a step more than imagining, you know. She didn't turn around at first because this felt nice, the hand on her. Then she turned around sharply and no one was there. It felt really bad now, the self-awareness. It had no substance or weight. It was like that mountain in *Through the Looking-Glass:* when she moved toward it, it got further away. She wanted furiously to be held then, as in the old slutty days. She looked at her trash compactor, and she wished there were a setting on it for being squeezed. She wanted to be squeezed into a tiny dot of flesh. Not killed, mind you. Squeezed and alive."

Malcolm sipped his wine ruminatively and said, "Aside from Lisa Cornerson being crazy, what interests me so far about this story is that you, Barbara, are able to know quite so many details about it."

"No," Barbara said definitively, "Lisa Cornerson is not crazy."

"And what about Barbara Sternberg?"

"Not only is Barbara Sternberg not crazy," said Barbara Sternberg. "Barbara Sternberg is the sanest person I know."

"Yes, but how is Barbara Sternberg able to tell this story with such certainty of the details if she wasn't actually there?"

"I was there when Lisa Cornerson leaned over the dinner table and told me these things as if she couldn't stop herself. If you had been there, you would remember every word." Looking at Malcolm, she squinted abruptly as if something— a new mole or birthmark—had just appeared on his face. "Actually, Malcolm, maybe you wouldn't."

"I want to hear what happens with Lisa and this guy," said Beth, the freelancer, gazing inadvertently at Rick Stein fidgeting in his chair.

"Lisa boarded the plane to Iowa on a Friday evening, worn out from two weeks of feeling a lot and thinking new thoughts. She looked around for the guy, who said he always took that same flight, didn't see him, sat down. She had developed a passion for looking out the airplane window. With her entire body she faced the window and noted every change in the area outside the window that she could see. She was entertained by this activity for hours, the way most people are entertained by the little porthole of television.

"She claims she noticed the man in the seat behind her first as a change in atmosphere. He asserted himself on her skin as coolness. Without turning around she said, 'You again?' being practiced in that kind of banter that both exposes your intentions and cloaks them. 'Yes and no,' he replied. She pictured his hand moving toward her hair in the way she remembered him moving—coming forward while kind of staying behind. She wondered if she was letting him touch her hair yet. She felt a cold tickle on the back of her neck and spun around. He was wearing a light blue worsted-wool suit this time, very soft. There was the same grayish blond hair, the pale gray skin, the gray eyes, she observed, carefully, because she knew soon she wouldn't have the presence of mind to observe anything. She was being sucked into the whirlpool.

"By the way, his hand had been nowhere near her hair. He was writing something on a piece of paper again—a verbal expression of the strain on his face, maybe. He handed her the paper. 'Please, let's go someplace private to talk when the plane lands. I won't ask to touch you.'

"She handed it back to him. The note said, 'I won't ask to touch you' and not 'I won't touch you.' She didn't look at him or talk to him for the rest of the plane ride. After the plane landed he looked even paler and more strained. Lisa was mulling over where her motel room was in relation to the motel manager's office, in terms of motel security. She told him where the motel was. 'Can you get there?' 'If I go right now with you.' 'No. Come tomorrow at six. I finish work at five. My name is Lisa Cornerson.' He told her his name—I can't remember it.

"He came early to the motel, before Lisa was ready for him. She scrambled to make them tea on the hot plate in the room. They sat down at the small round table by the west-facing picture window. The sun was setting, and the strong orange light had an effect on the man. It gave him a distinct outline. His blue worsted-wool suit looked crisper. It was easier to tell how old he was now. He was thirty-eight, Lisa guessed. She was thirty then.

" 'So, tell me about your mother,' Lisa said, sort of as a joke. He was startled by that. His face took on an expression of alarm all of a sudden but also by degrees, like an event and a slow-motion instant replay of the event happening at the same time. She wondered if she was in love. Now the man

looked down at his lap, and she sensed he had become sad. A
minute or two went by in silence. Lisa wasn't really scared.

"He looked up and smiled. She could see that she was
going to get an anecdote. 'I was not born in the normal way,'
he said. 'Something went wrong. I was not born all in one
place. I broke up into tiny pieces and seeped out every available hole in my mother. Birth for me was a kind of death.'
'Okay,' Lisa said. He said, 'Me—the baby—I—was thousands
of tiny particles, like a cloud. Imagine that. Your body is
thousands of little bodies. This is where my mother helped
me—you asked about my mother. She gathered me together
and held me. And when she held me I felt unified, because I
loved her, because all of me loved her. Loving her was the
form I occupied. You know what's funny, Lisa?' That was the
first time he said her name, and to Lisa, her own name was
the strangest thing the man had said. 'It's what I don't remember about that time in my life that scares me the most.'

" 'I understand that.' 'What?' 'You have a memory and
you don't know what it is.' 'That happens to you?' 'Yes.' 'Wow.
You're really nice.'

"Now, you might think somewhere in here was the golden
opportunity to ask him what the hell he was talking about,
was he out of his mind, but she was just happy he was talking.
It made the trippy feeling go away. 'So,' she said, 'you seem
like this normalish guy. Not a cloud anymore, I mean. What

happened?' 'I became a boy, then a teenager, then a man.' 'And your mother?' 'I loved my mother, but I don't think my mother loved me.' 'That's really sad.' 'I wanted her to know how happy I had once been, before I was born, so every year on her birthday I gave her gifts of darkness.'

"Now the trippy feeling came back, and Lisa closed her eyes. 'I'm sorry, I don't think I know what that is. What is that—a gift of darkness?'

"When he didn't respond, she opened her eyes. He was no longer sitting at the table. She felt a coolness on her shoulders, and then something cool and soft spread out over her scalp, and this was just right because the tea and the sunlight had made her feel hot. 'Are you touching me now?' she asked. Still the man said nothing. Lisa laughed again, and this time she really couldn't stop. This was the drunken Lisa coming back to visit. In a single minute, she felt as if she were disgorging hours of drunken laughter.

" 'It's okay,' the man said. 'I won't ask to take your clothes off. This won't be adultery, I promise.' 'I'm not married,' she said. His touch spread out over her back and her arms. When he touched her breasts through her shirt, she heard a noise somewhere else in the room. She tried to ignore the noise, because he was touching her so nicely. She stood up and turned around to face him. He was gritting his teeth, and his face looked strained again. She put her hands on his shoulders. 'What was that noise?' she said. 'What noise?' 'It sounded like someone moaning in pain.' 'That was you.'

"Lisa found herself down on the motel carpet. She and the man were stretched out inside a long parallelogram of sunlight. She closed her eyes. She couldn't figure out exactly where he was touching her at any given moment, though she did feel the vibrations of the sounds she was making in her chest and throat, unless that was also him, touching her in those places. 'Tell me,' he said, 'what this feels like to you.' 'I can't.' 'Yes you can.' 'I don't do that. I'm not a big talker while—' 'Please. Please.' Silence. 'I said, please tell me. Tell me. Tell me!' 'No, stop it, get off of me, get your hands off of me.'

"He did. He stopped when she asked him to stop. She stood up and walked around the room a little and looked at mundane things—the table, the minifridge, the teacups. She sat down at the table and said with an ironic edge, 'All right, so give me an example of a "gift of darkness." '

" 'The first gift of darkness I gave my mother was nighttime. I was just a child. She laughed at me, sort of the way you were just laughing. She said anyone could have given her that, and besides, she wanted a gift she could have during the day. So I gave her a black tree with five leaves. She didn't like that either. She neglected the tree. It died. When I was ten years old, I removed everything from my bedroom and boarded up the windows. I invited her in on the morning of her birthday, which happened to be a sunny morning. I hoped this would be like inviting her into her own womb. She said, "What's so special about this?" That was too much for me. I cried and I couldn't stop crying. "You're a terrible burden to me," she said, and then, "Oh, no, I didn't mean that. That's not true. I don't know why I said that. I'm so sorry. Sweetheart, you come here now." She took me in her arms in my dark, empty bed-room with boards on the windows. It was almost the same as if she had liked the gift. I felt if I could give her a gift that truly pleased her, she would love me like that all the time. I lined every inch of my room with black plastic and filled my room with water. I invited my mother and father into the room. They came into the room and they were suspended in the dark water, and they were happy. Submerged in my bedroom, they danced around and around in circles. There was only one thing left to do. For the most radiant darkness, I threw the light switch and electrocuted my parents.'

"The man was touching Lisa again, and she had become lost in the way he was touching her. 'My father died,' said the man, 'and my mother was horribly disfigured. Her body shriveled up, and her head grew enormous and bumpy and grotesque. I emptied the water from my room. My mother could not leave the house anymore because she had become a monster. I kept her in my black room without furniture, and once a day I brought her food and water. She loathed me.' By now he was touching Lisa relentlessly. His hands were cold and damp, and he rubbed them against her skin so it almost hurt. She looked up at him, and his face was contorted, hateful. He himself looked disfigured, and he hissed at her: ' "You! You." ' She stood up and told him to leave. He left, just like that, before she could say anything else, such as 'Come back.'

"Lisa sat at the table in the motel room for a long while. She couldn't figure out what time it was because the sky was lighter than when the man had arrived. Ten o'clock, her watch said. She went to the motel office and bought a paper and went back to her room. After she had been reading the paper for a while she noticed it was Monday's paper. So she had been alone in the room with the guy from Saturday evening to Monday morning. Missed her plane. Should have been at work by now, sending out art to the color separators, or whatever. Her own mother had just died, so she understood the story the man told her about his mother. Weighed down by her life yet unattached to her life, this (him, the room, the sunlight), she now felt, is what she had been waiting for; first the drinking and sexual sprees, followed by the print-manager job, the daily commute into the city, the moderate friendships, the gardening—all of them ways to hold herself down on the earth so she wouldn't float away before she could get to this.

"She took a shower that was uncomfortable because of how the water rattled against her skin. She tried to remember what she was thinking the last time she was thinking clearly. That must have been before six o'clock on Saturday. Or maybe it was two weeks ago. Maybe longer. Maybe never. At least with the gardening there were familiar things: a round, green tomato, a lumpy green haricot vert, that soft brown stuff—dirt. A motel room ought to be familiar but isn't. It has a table, a bed, a door, but they always read like jokes. If it's a motel, you can count on the cheesiness of the materials, like hack regional theater. You have furniture without comfort, you have sex without love. Whether you're committing adultery or not, if you're in a motel it's almost obligatory that you fall into a state of despair.

"Lisa walked out into the parking lot in a T-shirt and jeans and her dark, wet hair. She was hunched over, maybe more than usual let's say. This was a huge blacktop parking lot an hour by car from Iowa City. Late October, wind blowing. Lisa Cornerson, hunched over in the Midwest. She was hunched over so the wind wouldn't scatter her across the big, flat parking lot. When the man had touched her he kind of loosened up the border of her skin. She crossed her arms. She jammed one ankle behind the other. The man had done a certain thing to her. You know, that thing. He had created a condition. He touched her and then he stopped touching her. So now she was standing in one place in the parking lot, and yet spreading out over the entire parking lot."

"When does she make the phone call?" It was Rick Stein asking.

"What phone call?" Barbara thought Rick Stein should just get it over with, admit he was in love with Beth Falco the freelance writer, and that would be two less people the world had to worry about.

"The phone call where she announces she's disappearing. Who'd she call, by the way?"

"She called her boss at the time, Tony Gold."

"Tony Gold!"

"Who's Tony Gold?" asked Linda Lazar.

"The story on Tony Gold was Tony Gold was this short, compact little pit bull from Brooklyn who used to boss everyone around, including his superiors," Rick Stein said enthusiastically. "He was always at work very early in the morning hunched over four-color with his lupe. At least his defenders said he was hunched over four-color with his lupe. His detractors said he was hunched over a mirror with a tightly rolled twenty-dollar bill up his nose. He had this way of walking into any room and hammering the people in the room with a speech about something—stereo equipment or your job performance. Do we remember this guy?"

"Rick—" Beth said.

"The story on Tony Gold is late one night he walked into the office of some art director, I can't remember this chick's name. He begins bossing her around, he works himself up into a froth of bossing her around until she picks up an X-Acto knife and stabs him in the heart. Well, not in the heart but in the heart area of his chest—in his compact little pectoral, in his tit!"

"Rick honey, okay, take it easy," Beth said, and Barbara thought, "Look at that, she's already talking to him like a wife. Are these two people going to wake up?"

"So what did Tony Gold do? He became flustered, kind of hysterical. He said, 'That's a firing offense, that's a firing offense!' Next morning? Tony didn't show up for work. He came in at noon, cleared out his desk, left the job. Was he fired? Did he quit? I happen to think he was fired through I don't know what kind of deal or blackmail that art director had going with somebody or other. The point is, poof! He was gone."

"This is all quite fascinating, Rick, but it's very late now and some of us want to find out what happened to Lisa Cornerson," Beth said.

" 'Lisa Cornerson was standing in the vast Midwestern parking lot, hunched over,' " Malcolm mocked.

"Thank you, Malcolm," Barbara said. "Lisa Cornerson in the parking lot. It was cold and windy, and she stood there a long time with wet hair and a T-shirt. Then she saw the man walking toward her from the edge of the parking lot, some aspect of his approach suggesting retreat. 'I walked a mile for these cigarettes,' he said, holding up a bright red box. The wind was pushing his thin hair all around his head. As he walked toward her, his blue suit was a few shades darker than the sky. 'It's cold out here, let's go inside,' he said. That was one of the happiest moments in Lisa's life."

"*That* was?" Malcolm said.

"Yes!" a couple of the women said.

"At the round table by the picture window in the motel room he lit a cigarette, inhaled, grabbed Lisa, and pulled her against him. He pressed his open mouth against hers, they made an airtight seal with their lips, and he blew the smoke into her mouth. Her eyes were closed, and she pictured this dark chamber of their two mouths with a pale cloud of smoke floating inside. Everything in the world went away except for the inside of their two mouths. This was their first kiss.

"Then he was undressing her on the bed. Then he was touching her again in that astonishing way, touching her all over at once. She was naked and lying on her back, and he knelt above her in his blue suit, brushing the tops of her thighs with his hands. It made her cry a little bit. She said, 'What are you doing? You're doing something different from before.' 'Before,' he said, 'I thought you didn't like what I was doing, because you wouldn't tell me how it felt to be touched, so I'm trying something different.' 'Oh, honey, you're just like a man after all. Don't get too self-conscious about it.' Then he got self-conscious. She needed a break because things were getting too intense. What she did during the break was she undressed him. This is the first time she was aware of touching him. His skin was oddly pliant. It almost seemed to shift away from the places where she put pressure on it. She knelt above him and touched his thighs. He let her do that for a while until he pulled her down onto him and they had what Lisa described as awkward sex, which, paradoxically, endeared him to her even more. She lay back and closed her eyes and felt the cool, unlocatable sensation of his hands gently on her skin again, and she knew she was in love with this man.

"They sat on the bed smoking cigarettes, though Lisa didn't normally smoke. 'Do you think I made up the stories I've told you?' he asked. 'No, I knew you were telling the truth,' she said."

Barbara said, "Who wants more wine? I have two more bottles of the Merlot."

Various people in the group expressed the sentiment, "Finish the damn story."

"That's basically it," Barbara said.

"What do you mean, 'That's basically it'?" Rick Stein said.

"What about the phone call?" asked Julia Katz, who was the other married woman.

"Oh yes, the phone call. Lisa and the man decided to get an apartment together in Iowa City. She called up Tony Gold on that same Monday and said, more or less, 'The press run was fine. I'm quitting as of right this second. I've moved away from the East Coast.' Word has it Tony Gold threw his phone across the room."

Barbara stood up and began clearing glasses. Everyone could see that she felt she was done for the evening and was doing the activities you do when you want to suggest to people that they should leave your apartment.

"And?"

"And the phone didn't even break."

"Why are you trying to beg off on the rest of this?" Beth Falco asked.

Now it was as if it were not Barbara who had been telling the story but some stranger who had barged into her house and held the floor; as if the story were a filibuster against the real event of the evening. "Because it's late," Barbara snapped.

Everyone was exhausted now, and suddenly all but one of them resented Barbara. This one—Malcolm Browning—was fascinated, a bemused smile on his face.

"Finish the story," Julia Katz said.

"They settled in Iowa City. She got a part-time job at National Color Press, where he worked. She took courses at the university and kept a vegetable garden. And she had a phantom lover, and every day this phantom lover came home from his job and he lit a cigarette and pressed his lips against hers and blew smoke down into her lungs. When she met him she was thirty. Eight years later she was diagnosed with chronic bronchitis. So he had to stop blowing smoke down into her lungs. So he left her."

"No!"

"Yeah, he did. He left her. Or maybe she left him."

"What? You can't do that. What's the matter with you, Sternberg? You build up this whole thing—"

"Look," Barbara said, "you can leave someone and still feel like you're the one who was left. The point is, eight years went by, the amount of time it takes to go from being young to being not so young anymore. She returned to her dead mother's house in Mount Vernon, and everything was broken and caked over with dust. She had gone on a long, dangerous trip and come back bereft and permanently injured."

Beth said, "I think a person always has the option of recovering from these events."

"Absolutely not. You're like a child, Beth."

"You are arrogant and narcissistic," Rick Stein said to Barbara. "You keep us here with this monologue, nobody else is allowed to talk, and now you abuse us."

"I didn't abuse you, I abused Beth."

"I resent this entire evening," Rick said.

"Boy, I guess it's time to go," said Julia Katz.

"Okay, maybe so," Linda Lazar said, and smiled sorrow-fully at Barbara.

Only Linda Lazar, out of everyone, kissed Barbara good night on the way out the door. She also held Barbara's glance for a moment, and touched Barbara's cheek.

Barbara stood at her window and watched everyone emerge onto the street several stories below. Rick Stein and Beth Falco got into separate cabs. "Idiots," Barbara thought, "can't even manage to get in the same cab." Linda and Julia, the two married women, lingered a moment on the sidewalk for a prolonged hug and kiss, to make Barbara wonder if this weren't one of those difficult and ambiguous arrangements people make with each other all at once by the seat of their pants, and then carry out in various compromised permuta-tions for the rest of their lives.

"Malcolm, honey," Barbara called. "Are you still here?"

Malcolm returned to the living room from the bathroom, where he had been hiding. She turned away from the window to face him. "So," she said, "won't your wife be waiting up for you?" She said this in the manner of an aphorism, a refrain, a running joke.

"Tonight's her bridge night," he replied in kind.

"Did you resent my story?"

"No. I liked your story very much."

"Did you think I was making it up?"

"No. I knew your story was true."

"I can tell you're lying," she said. He had approached her, and they were standing side by side, facing out into the living room, silhouetted by the window.

"I'm not lying. I'm troubled, though. Is there no innocence? Even the baby in that story was a mean, lustful baby. My baby boy is not like that. I take him to the park in his stroller and we see another baby and I say, 'Look! A baby!' and he says, 'A baby!' and he's just so happy."

"Malcolm. Do you think I'll ever be happy?"

"No."

"Malcolm?"

"Yes?"

"I know you can't stay over, but would you come and tuck me into bed?"

"Okay, sweetheart."

Malcolm walked Barbara to her bedroom. She undressed herself in front of him and put on her purple silk pajamas. He walked up behind her and removed the elastic band from her lovely hair, which fell about her shoulders. She climbed into bed, and he pulled the covers up to her chin.

"I'm very sleepy now."

"You've had a hard night."

"Would you sit here on the edge of the bed and watch me fall asleep? It won't take long, I promise."

"Okay."

"Good night, Malcolm."

"Good night, Lisa Cornerson."

She smiled and closed her eyes, and Malcolm remained seated on the edge of her bed until she was breathing the way he knew she breathed when she was asleep. Malcolm stood up very quietly and let himself out of her apartment. When she heard the latch click, Barbara opened her eyes, and was the tiniest bit glad they had all finally gone.

In the Snowy Kingdom

A handsome young couple is dressing in their boudoir for a black-tie fundraiser at which the woman will speak:

ANNOUNCER, VOICE-OVER: Strong enough for a man but made to help keep a woman dry.
MAN: You know, I wouldn't mind if we were the only ones there.
WOMAN: Then you better bring your checkbook.

—TV advertisement for antiperspirant

HERE SHE WAS, GLITTERING. FROM A TABLE AT THE BACK OF the large ballroom in the midtown hotel, he saw her upper torso and her head above all the other heads at the fundraiser. She was up there with her nervous shoulders, her smooth, lightly powdered throat, her diamond necklace, the coiled potential of her long raven hair. As she gave her speech, the words drifted past his head like a gentle wind. The reassuring cadences of this speech tonight were the very ones that calmed him when she lay on top of him at home on the living room rug during his attacks of nerves. He knew the checks would come out of the pocketbooks tonight, the redundant and comforting certainty of the fundraiser. Her bright, soft shoulders. He felt peaceful and tingly.

Most of the top executives in his firm had come. There was Bosquet, one of the other young VPs, several tables in front of him, his favorite VP aside from himself, a good egg, handsome, with impeccable Nixonian hair. He himself had never been able to deploy hair gel in a comely arrangement.

His hair was too light in color maybe, and with the gel it had appeared too greasy, or alternately greasy and dry in patches. He liked Bosquet. Good feeling toward all fellowmen, fellow-persons.

But something had gone wrong. Bosquet was staring at him. Of the 150 people at the black-tie fundraiser, 135 were staring at him. He looked up at his wife onstage. One of her bare, white, hairless arms had been amputated, except there was still a hand at the end of it; but the hand was attached to this little stubby arm. His throat closed up. Sweat poured down from inside his head of light brown hair. He needed a set of keys to grip tightly in his hand, but she had all the keys and, come to think of it, his checkbooks. He looked up at her again and realized that the shortness of her arm was an optical illusion: her arm appeared foreshortened because she was pointing it directly at him. "Dan?" she asked. She had finished her speech and was asking him to do something.

"Stand up," she said.

Later, in the cold Arctic motel, he would wonder what had brought on the paralysis. Everyone was looking at him, and he couldn't make his legs move. He laughed. His hair was wet as if he had just gone swimming. He urinated freely down his trouser leg. Lacking keys, he gripped his wineglass until it broke in his hand. Blood dripped from his fingertips. He wanted his wife to cover for him—"Oh, I guess he's too modest to stand up"—and make her closing remarks. He knew it was really the deep, death-bound devotion of a good marriage, and not some hostile, jealous drive to embarrass him that made her step from behind the podium, jump down off the stage in her black pumps, and rush toward him with tears in her eyes. Still, he would make her pay for it.

"Darling," she said, in the ballroom, while everybody watched. She had his face in her hands, and to the extent that he could forget where he was, which was not much, he was comforted and aroused by the touch of her fingers. He beckoned her ear toward his mouth. He had meant to whisper something but found himself gently licking her ear. There appeared on her face the outward display of the most deeply felt confusion he had ever seen, followed by what looked like, in facial vocabulary, the realization that she had done something wrong. Meanwhile, sixty people were on their feet in a tight, dense circle around Dan, who was seated in his own urine, and Tara, who was bending over him in her tight dress with her soft, fragrant shoulders. He whispered his request. Those people nearest his mouth heard only the word "ice," and Tara felt awful as she steeled herself to abide.

AFTER BUYING THE WHEELCHAIR AND THE SKINS TO COVER THEIR bodies and a half-dozen pairs of silk long underwear apiece, they made the journey by airplane and car to the northern-most motel in the world. Tara noticed that flight attendants and porters and cab drivers spoke loudly and slowly to Dan, as if it were his brain that was screwed up. She almost quit the journey several times because it was so hard for her to ma-neuver his lame body from a taxicab back into his wheelchair or, say, from his wheelchair onto an airplane toilet seat. She was sure it was in retribution for embarrassing him at the fundraiser that he made her haul his entire weight again and again, as often as possible, making, all the while, maddening jokes, such as, "I'm pregnant" or "Who ever knew a person could be *this* pregnant?" or "I'm Roosevelt."

The first hours in the motel room, which they did not in-tend to leave for two weeks, were taken up with free-floating mutual panic and affectionate hostility. "I can't believe I made you do this," Dan said. "Now you're gonna leave me."

"No. Don't say that. Those are not acceptable words be-tween us even as a joke or, I don't know, a salvo. If there's any-thing that will make me leave you, it's if you say *that* again."

The motel room was big, with cheap orange furniture and small windows on two walls looking out upon harsh, bright ice and snow. There was a kitchenette with stained cookware and a queen-size bed, the head of which was flush with one of the windowless walls. Overall it was pale and forty-seven degrees in this room.

"I'm cold," she said.

"Burn some money," he said. "This was such a bad idea. We've got to get out of here."

"No, we're staying. I'd love to stay here and take care of you."

"You would?" he whimpered happily, sitting up in the middle of the bed. "It's such a strain just to sit up. I'm gonna flop over any second."

"So lean against the wall."

"I can't."

"You're pathetic," she said, the beginning of a flirtation. "I married you because you were tall and brawny and handsome."

He wanted to say something really mean in reply, perhaps how she bored him sexually (not true), but he knew the full ethical power of this two-week-long reproach rested on not forming certain things in words.

She put on a mink coat. "I'm cold," he said.

"Are you cold all over or just from the waist up?"

"Waist up."

She laughed. She ran across the room and leapt from the floor directly onto his shoulders, knees first. She pinned his shoulders to the bed with her knees. His arms went numb. He couldn't do a thing. She reached behind her and unzipped his fly. "Oh no, don't do that, that's a really bad idea, I don't want to find out whether *that's*—oh. Oh my. Oh yes, do that. Wow, that is incredible."

She climbed off him and went to inspect the kitchen. "Hey!" he said.

"I guess the invalid-swain combination is not a turn-on," she said.

"I didn't know you could be this cruel."

"*You* didn't know *I* could be this cruel?"

She walked by the bed and he tried to grab her. She dodged him easily.

———————

IN THE MORNING, COLD AIR TRESPASSED UPON THEIR UNHAPPY dreams. They lay in bed a long time with their eyes open, not looking at one another, dreading the temperature and their confinement.

"Oh my God!" Tara said.

"What?"

"Look at your feet."

"Where are they?"

"Standard foot location."

"I can't find them. Describe them to me."

"They're blue."

"Are they not under the skins?"

"No."

"Do you think there's permanent damage?"

She lifted the heavy skin they were using as a blanket and slid her body out from under it. She stood at the foot of the bed in her full set of rainbow silk thermal attire, her dark, un-combed hair scattered about her shoulders. She pressed her palms to the soles of his cold feet and shoved his feet back under the skins. "Did you feel anything when I did that?"

"What did you do?"

"Jerked you off."

"Very funny."

She made coffee and defrosted some bagels and put them on the rusty bridge table where they foresaw eating all their meals for the next two weeks. She spent half an hour hauling her husband's inert body out of bed, dressing it, and placing it in the wheelchair at the bridge table. He ate the naked bagel and drank the coffee—both of which had long ago gone cold and lost what little taste pleasure they might once have given—without uttering a word of complaint or gratitude.

"This is like having a baby. This is good practice for hav-ing a baby," she said from somewhere behind him in the room. "You can't move, I satisfy all your needs, you're not grateful, you're a useless blob."

"What are you doing back there?"

"Writing a letter."

"To whom?"

"My mother."

"What does it say?"

" 'Dear Mom, I'm in the Arctic with Dan. I know I haven't asked you for advice since that summer when I was ten years old and you threw up your arms in despair and sent me to that awful, lecherous psychiatrist, but it seems Dan's legs are paralyzed and he told me he wants him and me to be the only two remaining people on the planet, he wants everyone else dead. At least that's what he whispered to me when his legs went limp in the Ritz-Carlton ballroom: "I want the world to be an Arctic desert." Did you and Dad ever go through this kind of thing? Please write soon. I love Dan, and I would do anything for him, anything, anything.' "

As she was reciting the letter, she saw in the half-open drawer of the cheap little blond-wood writing desk a small crowbar. When she came to the word "anything," she thought of running toward her husband and slamming the back of his head with the crowbar. "There's a crowbar in the drawer," she said.

"Most motels put Bibles."

"What do you think it's for?"

"What are you wearing?"

"Gray cardigan sweater; black lycra ski pants, tight; big fluffy brown slippers."

"Hair?"

"Up."

"Face?"

"Set."

"Eyebrows?"

"Plucked."

"Ears?"

"Fucked."

"What's the weather like outside?"

"Are you blind now too?"

"My neck is stiff."

"I'm going to write letters. I don't know what else to do."

"What? I can't hear you. I'm deaf."

"Don't make so many jokes. I can't handle this many jokes."

"You're not allowed to write letters. Everyone you're writing to is dead."

"That's too horrible. Why do you insist on that?"

"I hate when you ask me why I do or feel certain things. Don't ever ask me 'why' anything."

"I have to write letters."

"What if you don't?"

"Then we have to leave."

"So this is going to be one of our compromises, one of the compromises of our marriage?"

"Pretty much we're in the Arctic and I'm writing letters, yes."

Dan woke up alone thinking of bosquet with the hair. Bosquet's hair had become an emblem of all the humiliations Bosquet had not suffered. The one enchantment Dan possessed—money, that a thousand banks could burn to the ground and Dan would laugh (if something were funny)— Bosquet also had. But it was Bosquet's lack of a public degradation in his life that Dan begrudged him, not his wealth. Dan did know that if you have a penny, I cannot also have that penny, which knowledge often bred in rich people an anxious competitiveness with other rich people, but Dan had transcended that. For one thing, he did not mistake wealth for wisdom. There had to be a certain attitude one acquired along with the money, a base level of spiritual attainment vis-à-vis money: call it the thousand-banks-burning serenity. Dan had that. But so did Bosquet. The question really was how Bosquet would hold up under a public urination. Dan thought that he himself was doing pretty well. Whispering the Arctic thing to Tara, that was a good split-second recovery, quarterback sneak-type thing. Anyway, wasn't this all really just a lark?

He heard the shower going in the bathroom. He pictured Tara bathing. He was furious that she had deserted him for the shower. In there tending to needs that were not his. He couldn't bear it. He wanted to die. He forced himself back down into sleep.

When he came up again she was gone. He screamed her name. No answer. All alone. Exactly how he had felt at the fundraiser. He had wanted never to feel so alone again. He screamed her name until he was hoarse. Then he threw off the skin and sat up and put on as many clothes as he could. He could not get any pants on over his legs, which were like two long, intractable meat loaves. He put on a full-length white fur coat and wheeled himself out the motel door. His wheelchair jammed in the ice, and he fell facedown on the ice. The air temperature was forty degrees below zero, Fahrenheit. He had no idea air could hurt a person this much. He dragged himself toward the motel office, twenty-five yards away across the ice. He thought he wouldn't survive, and it was his own fault for treating Tara as a servant, like the guy who is mean to his dog in Jack London's "To Build a Fire." He couldn't believe how much pain. He grabbed the ice with his mittens and grappled forward, forward, forward to the motel office.

He wriggled across the threshold of the motel office. The motel office was so luxurious that he thought he either had arrived at the motel office or was dead. The silver carpet was so expensive! The moose on the wall. Tara shouting into the telephone: "Bosquet! Bosquet I love you! Please, Bosquet!"

"No!" Dan was on his belly in the doorway.

"Dan," she said, startled. Now the knowledge ran all through him that had been stored until now in his dead legs. She dropped the phone and rushed to him. Again, rushing was a kind of mistake. Why hurry now? He was not angry. He gave in to his pathetic love for Tara. She stood directly above him and saw his teardrops repelled by the thick, soft, brown, waterproofed leather of her snow boots.

———————

THE SKIN ON THE BED WAS STINKY NOW. TARA AND DAN WERE beneath it, weeping from the cold. Encountering the air out of doors had been like throwing themselves down repeatedly on something hard. They lay loosely touching hands, recuperating. Tara's arms were shot and her back severely wrenched: she had fireman-carried Dan back from the motel office.

"I'm breaking under the strain," she said. "There's something you don't understand about my being up here with you," she said. "Your success, you know, your success is immanent in you. You are your success. If you are here, it is here, even if you are a cripple. My success is the way I am in contact with other people."

"Other people. What am I, chopped liver?"

"I think you know what I mean. You can separate the two, your success and the world. I can't."

Dan discovered that despite the mind-boggling, unassimilable betrayal in the motel office, he could still listen to his wife, or think he was listening. "I know," he said. "Your success depends on your keeping in touch with your community."

"No, my success *is* keeping in touch with my community," Tara said. "You know, Dan, I've realized something on our journey. The way you and I are together—call it the North Pole way of being together—I'm the cripple in that. You think if you just throw money at me I won't also need a life. I can't stay here two weeks."

"Let me just send up a flare over here in this conversation," he said. "Half an hour ago I crawled into the office as you were telling Bosquet you love him, or was I hallucinating?"

"Oh, that?"

"Here we go, ladies and gentlemen."

"First of all, I'm offended that you think what you're thinking. Second, I'm really sorry that you had to go through a half hour of your life believing I had deceived and betrayed you. I was trying to call *anyone* from that phone. I really did feel as if they had all died. The first person I got through to was Helena Bosquet, only Helena wasn't home, Bosquet was. So I just—he became, don't you see, the representative of everyone out there. I poured it into his ear, my love for all of them." (This happened to be true—it just felt to her like a lie as she was saying it.) "It was crazy, I know. I'm going crazy up here."

Dan believed Tara with all his heart, and something was happening to him that had never happened before. His heart was really melting. "You're right," he said. "My love has been all wrong. We have to get out of here. We must go back and apply the world to our wounded selves like a gigantic poultice."

"Oh, Dan!"

They hugged each other hard, and, an instinctive overture, she ran her fingers lightly across his thighs. He felt them. They were now complete. They were the couple who had everything. He moved his legs toward hers, and they held each other in a tight embrace.

"Now let's get out of here."

"I agree."

They lay another fifteen minutes under the skins, holding each other. They had logged important relationship time under these skins, and they wondered if they ought to hollow out an area of their house—storage, this was usually called, the attic, the junk closet, "the crawl space, honey"—and develop the flotsam of a career in love, as in, "I can't believe we still have *this*. Imagine, the things we thought worth saving. We save *everything*."

"Come on, really, you get out of bed first, Mr. Paralysis."

"I can't."

"Stop."

"Can't move."

"Please. It's been nice, but I gotta get outta here."

"Can't move anything now. Arms."

"Danny, cut it out."

"It spread." He wasn't kidding. The paralysis was back, and it had spread.

She turned her head and took a big piece of his biceps and gnashed it. "You feel that?"

"Feel what?"

"All right, I'm at peace with this. We'll see if this lasts. My peace, that is. I think it will. I feel different now."

"We can still try to leave if you want."

"Don't be stupid."

Dan had some limited neck movement available, and he turned his head enough to see her face above the discolored blanket of skin. Her face had become naturally pale, resembling her soft, lightly powdered face on the night of the fundraiser. Bright, soft, cloudy Arctic light came in through the windows. "Let me see your shoulders," he said.

She climbed out on top of the skins, naked. She had bathed quite recently, and all her skin was pale and clean and glowed from within like some pagan marble orb. Her body was full, whole, unforeshortened as she crawled around above him on the bed, as if a woman were meant to be seen by her husband only in this strictly polar condition of light. Gradually she allowed every aspect of her breasts to be touched by his tongue, over which he retained intricate muscular control. He was able to notice with his tongue the way that her breasts emerged cleanly and roundly from the rest of her torso and the way that her nipples, distinct, round unto themselves, repeated in miniature the grand formal movement of her breasts. She presented her shoulders for the slow inspection of his tongue. He was face-up on the bed. She stood and yanked him by the ankles so that his feet and lower legs hung off the side and his wet tongue, so far the only mobile organ, was situated at the geographic center of the bed. She moved the surface of her belly over this remarkable small wet writhing organism barnacled to the dead mass of her husband. When it became dry she let it spread out and water in her labia, and then she gave it her inner thighs to work on, and her knees, and her calves, and her ankles, and the arches of her feet, and her toes, and back up to her thighs, and this was no easy work for her, and she was gasping with the effort. Again there was this need for watering, and she let his squirmy tongue dawdle in her crotch, and she sort of relaxed and hummed and sighed, rearranging herself now and then over his tongue, which was still soaking in the necessary liquids. In one of these rearrangements she noticed his penis, too, was in working order, and now she was not relaxed, she was frantic, scrambling, and very soon she managed to lower herself down onto the penis. A few fast, easy lowerings and raisings caused an uncontrollable shaking in all her muscles, and she huddled down on him for tighter, stronger movements and grabbed some part of his impassive flesh with her teeth and hands for a few last moments of deep, squalling effort and release.

She flopped forward and sprawled on him for a while. Then she peeled herself back and ran to the steaming hot shower, leaving him supine and naked on the bed. He knew some extraordinary expenditure had just been made by himself because he was panting, which he experienced only as hot air leaving his mouth in short gusts and cold air coming in.

———————

FOR THE NEXT SEVERAL DAYS, EVERY PART OF HER BODY SHE could get his tongue on, she did. During this major industrial exposure to flesh, his tongue lost some of its delicacy. At times it was beyond parched—a swollen and seared meat. Tara took swigs of tap water from the motel kitchen sink without swallowing, knelt above him all hot and bothered, carried her mouth down to his dry spot, poured her water there, and then used his tongue to paste the water once more all over her skin before climbing onto his erect cock, up and down fast and good with low hums and high curdling little cries at the end. She had taken to springing up immediately after sex and racing to the hot motel shower while Dan remained naked and dazed on the stripped motel bed, his flesh covered with large, pointy goose bumps to which he was completely oblivious.

Having aired her objections to the oppressive twosome, Tara no longer feared her husband, at least not while he was 98 percent immobilized. Whatever else this was, it had now also become a sensual vacation. For several days of their marriage, the long lick and quick fuck were the only things Dan was not impotent to do. But he was impotent not to do them, which may have been why, one cold afternoon while inadvertently working himself up into a frenzy in their snowy vaginal kingdom built for two, Dan noticed his mouth was uttering a string of words particularly masculine and foul, culminating with that bad, blunt word referring to a certain part of his wife's body.

Tara felt the whole long, sick Arctic weekend build up in her at once. She took the crowbar out of the drawer of the cheap blond-wood desk, raised it above her head, and then threw it on the orange nappy rug in disgust. She said she would leave the motel because she didn't want to kill him. She also said she would leave the marriage. She left. In the motel office, with nothing more than vehement talk and seventy thousand dollars in cash, she persuaded the motelier to give her his four-wheel-drive vehicle, whose motor had been running in perpetuity since date of purchase, because once you stop a motor in country this cold the vehicle becomes part of the landscape. She drove away.

Dan managed somehow to throw himself off the bed. Dragging himself forward by means of his chin, he arrived after an hour at the crowbar on the carpet. There he burst into tears for not being able to split his own skull in two. In another two hours, he had cried himself to sleep.

WHEN HE WOKE UP HE WAS NAKED AND FREEZING COLD. HE jumped to his feet and ran to the motel shower, where he let the scalding water soak into his skin for a long time. When he was dried and dressed he realized he could kill himself. He didn't want to anymore, but he did whip the crowbar into his own head in an effort to beat himself unconscious. He hit hard and didn't drop. There must have been a Darwinian mechanism that kept a man from knocking his own self out cold with a hand-held object.

While Dan was beating the crap out of his head, Tara motored southward in the 4WD despite morbid second thoughts and a blight on her future. She tried to go on, but her hands were shaking badly and she was sweating and she felt woozy, almost in sympathy with Dan, who by now had smashed his face with the crowbar so often that the skin had folded in over his eyes. Tara pulled a U-turn on the highway. Dan, body awareness at an all-time low, had missed his head with the crowbar the last few times and had taken instead to bending over every minute or so and wailing on his shins with the hard piece of metal.

Tara walked in.

"Dan!"

"Tara!"

"Your legs!"

"You've come back!"

———

THEY SAT ON THE BED AND EXCHANGED VOWS. HE BEGGED HER TO walk him to the car immediately. She stood up and tried to help him to his feet, and he said, "My legs, they've gone dead again. Just kidding!" He sprang to his feet, his eyes covered with swollen flesh.

In the motel office Tara bought Dan some cheapo sunglasses, and they set off in the vehicle.

"What checkbooks do you have on you?" she asked while driving.

"Chemical, Manny Hanny, Citibank."

"How much money total?"

"Whatever the FDIC limit is for each. Two hundred thousand, I guess."

"Sign me three checks for two hundred thousand each. Clean yourself out. Now."

"What? Why?"

"Because, you see, that's going to be our arrangement. You keep giving me a lot of money, and I never leave you."

"What are you going to do with the money?"

"It doesn't matter. Throw big fundraisers. Anything I want."

"What if I don't give you the money?"

"That's not part of the arrangement. You do give it, is the point. The other is not a logical category. 'I don't give you the money'—no truth value in that. You see?"

"Yeah."

"Start writing checks."

"I can't see."

"Do your best."

And so they drove back to boring old New York.

The Woman Who

A woman is seated in a movie theater. We hear:

I wanna be loved by you
Alo-o-one, poo-poo-pee-doo.

—TV advertisement for perfume

THERE WAS A WOMAN WHO LITERALLY TURNED INTO A MOVIE star. She remained in that state for two hours in a movie theater and then went back to being herself. The movie, which she had gone to see with friends, featured the star that the woman turned into. She went into the theater resembling her friends, and then this thing happened. She didn't become the star by being imbued suddenly with all of Her memories and feelings. She did, in a matter of ten seconds, like the blooming of a succulent tulip on speeded-up film, come to look exactly like Marilyn Monroe.

That was the first of a series of profound transformations in the life of Hazel Hess. The second, technically, was turning back into herself, when the credits rolled and the lights came up.

Before any of this happened she was just Hazel Hess, feeling constrained, not sure why. Part of the reason: she was—or felt she was—so much like a lot of other people. She was deeply tuned in to the stylistics of the educated urban women of her generation; that was the group she was a part of, and constrained by, and that much of the constraint in her life she knew about. She was an executive at a large fragrance and skin-care company, with a background in graphic design and art history. Married once, divorced once—no point going into that. Late thirties.

She looked like them, dressed like them, walked like them, ate and talked and thought like a lot of other people in her same area of the milieu. It's not that her thoughts were identical to theirs, but they came in similar phrases that were oriented toward the same ten thousand facts. She was smart enough to know she was trapped, but not smart enough to learn which kind of trap it was, and free herself, or so she thought: a dreary chain of thoughts, which had been with her for years.

Nobody special in her life right now. Dina Truro was her best friend. There was a good, strong, solid circle of other friends, some of them dating as far back as high school. Dina was the most dependable. Was that hard-wired? Things were set up that way. All of these good people and only one of them the best—a dozen bridesmaids, one maid of honor. Something sad in that.

She had thick, dark hair that she cropped short and pomaded. Big brown eyes, pale skin. She wore white a lot, at least in the immediate area surrounding her face. White blaz-

ers and frocks, pearl-drop earrings, thick white lycra head-
bands on the weekend. Ironically, she was more of an Audrey
Hepburn.

"Oh Trudy," she once said, "oh Trudy, Trudy, Trudy," for
that was what she called Dina Truro; sipping vodka martinis
on a couch loosely covered with pale linen in the lounge of a
fancy midtown hotel.

On the day it happened, Hazel Hess and a group of her
friends, walking up Fifth Avenue toward the revival house; a
mixture of her stylish friends, a pride of powerful women,
heading for the Monroe retrospective on a cold winter day.
There were men in there too, husbands and dates, the men
who had been near these women all their adult lives. This was
the tight circle of girlfriends, and these were the men con-
tingent to them, businessmen mostly, powerful also, each in
his own sphere, but secondary here. Men comfortable
enough to know when they were necessary extras, and feel
okay about it: that's a kind of beauty in a woman's life, deluxe
and soulful.

Hazel Hess feeling like an armature now, part of this apparatus of women, faceless aspect of an army of fashion,
sweeping up Fifth Avenue, razing everything in its path.
That's what it felt like anyway, in the sense that if this were a
movie, the group of women would be one choreographed
mass of furs and leathers and starkly defined faces in the

foreground, and everyone else on Fifth Avenue would be a blur going by. Hazel Hess was the background within the foreground, maybe because Dina "Trudy" Truro was with her fiancé, away from Hazel in another part of the pack, and Hazel herself was alone. In Hazel's private movie of this day, Hazel was not the heroine, she was just somewhere in there. "It's a mistake to think yourself the center of anything," Hazel thought—someone's affections, for example (but now we're getting into the area of her failed marriage). "It's a mistake," Hazel thought, turning west now onto Fifty-seventh Street, with some sadness, to think of hierarchy at all. Well, maybe not a mistake but a disappointment. Cold gust of wind. Hazel buttoned the top button of her red woolen coat, being quietly antifur; not as a political stance but again, to be not the center, not even of her own sense of luxury and comfort. Always leave something to be desired, could have been her motto. But we're not talking about a passive or self-effacing woman here. At work she made fifty significant decisions a day. She told people what to do all the time as a matter of course and without blinking. That was natural. You told people what to do because that's what you did and you were right. Your instincts were perfect every time.

Dark-haired Hazel Hess, drifting along Fifty-seventh Street like the light snow, first of the season. Two blocks away was the hard, almost colorless earth of Central Park, the actual earth. Hazel had no idea what was about to happen to her. It made sense that it would happen now though, in this rather dull stretch of her life. It marked the end of the dull stretch, a long dull stretch beginning about two years after the divorce, continuing even now on Fifty-seventh Street, about to end with a bang. Dull, not unhappy—the two years that followed the divorce, those were unhappy. These other years, about five of them, were just unextraordinary; okay, grim, too. Working, socializing, carrying on an agile life of mental nourishment that consisted of books and films and conversation and—why not?—the work in fragrance and skin care.

The twelve of them spread out over three rows in the darkened movie house. Deep red—the traditional color of movie houses forever and ever: plush seats, deep red curtains, glittering cut-glass chandeliers below a bas-relief red paisley ceiling. Waiting and chatting. Can you have a very serious discussion in the five minutes preceding *Gentlemen Prefer Blondes*? The movie was a layered in-joke. Who knew all the levels of irony and heartfelt sentiment in it? Possibly no one. Irony, sentiment, irony, sentiment, irony, sentiment: a good joke like a big cake.

Hazel alone refused to get the joke today. She wanted to hold the movie close to her like a warm hug from Mom. Hazel's mother was not the person to care about any such hugs; she had gotten to that point bitter cerebral prefeminist old mothers get to of not having a body, just about. "This? It's in my way, so I feed it. That's all," Hazel's mother might say. She wouldn't say that about Hazel, she would say it about her own body.

Hazel alone: that was Hazel today. Separated and isolated, like a thirteen-year-old aboriginal boy about to undergo some Gothic and horrifying rite of passage.

The lights went down, and the movie came on.

———————

DURING THE PERIOD OF HER LIFE FOLLOWING THE MOVIE, WHEN droves of seekers and supplicants came to her house, Hazel developed idiosyncratic ways of sharing her coveted Marilynness. She could make a person feel a certain way by dressing a certain way. Occasionally, in private audience with a Monroe pilgrim, she lifted a pinkie finger and the whole thing was over. At first she was overwhelmed when all the people began showing up at her house—who were they? where did they come from? how did they *know*?—but these people generally got what they wanted from her and left, and she was no worse for the wear. Besides, it was interesting.

Early in this period, after a typical day of work, there was someone to spend the evening with, if that was what she wanted. Most often that person was Dina Truro. Hazel began her workday at eleven or noon and continued to receive until about eight P.M. Then Dina or someone would show up. The two of them would shop for a savory meal, cook, sip cognac, talk about this new life.

"Who cleans your apartment, by the way?"

"I do," Hazel said.

"It's spotless."

"It's important to create an atmosphere."

"Spotless and just so."

"Like that."

"The chartreuse couch, the robin's-egg walls, the other couch in blue seersucker. A blue seersucker couch, for all year round, who would have thought?" Dina said meditatively.

"Yeah."

"All this stuff was here before though, wasn't it?"

"Yeah."

"It seems different now."

"I know."

"Is it just me, or are you keeping it really warm in here?"

"I am. It's part of the feeling. Cold winter out there, warm hearth in here. So warm you get a little confused, you don't know where you are, you drift, you dream, you're floating on a moonbeam. I almost never go out anymore. I wear white gloves in the morning."

"Your whole look."

"Typically I'll wear a dark blue dress, almost like a mohair, fairly low cut, choker of pearls. Silk scarf on my head, though I almost never go out. And have you noticed I'm keeping the hair longer these days?"

"Are you trying to be more like Marilyn?" Dina said, knowing she had missed the point.

"I'm going for Grace Kelly. An older Grace Kelly than we think of when we think of Grace Kelly."

"When you think of someone who would know how to receive people, you think of Grace Kelly. Marilyn was a slob, I would guess, though I haven't read any of the biographies. Have you?"

"Nope."

"What else?"

"I want to look old and feel old when I'm receiving, like someone decrepit whose mind is sharp as a whip."

"That's weird, because you look more like me."

"Yes. I'm trying to look like that sad comedienne from *The Dick Van Dyke Show.* I bet she went home after a day of comedy writing and drank herself into a stupor. Rose Marie. Was that the actress's name or the character's name?"

Dina, who was five years older than Hazel, felt the Rose Marie stuff was directed at her. She got morose and resentful. Hazel didn't notice—she was wise, not omniscient; in fact after these long days she was a little spaced-out.

"Oh!" Dina said, and spilled a drop of cognac on the blue couch.

"Here, let me get that." Hazel hopped up like a young hostess and poured salt on the spill, then wiped it away with water. "Did you have a sudden insight, hon?"

"No. I just remembered something. A man."

"Oh God."

"He's coming here tomorrow, a beautiful saxophonist. I've told him about you, and he's fascinated."

"Oh, a musician. So, a reliable man with lots of money."

"Please. He's just coming here the way everyone else comes here." The oracle thing was a bit of a strain on the friendship.

"Good. I'll turn up the heat even higher. I'll lift a pinkie finger for him."

"He'll die."

"So how's Jim?"

"Fine."

"Have you two set a date yet?"

"Shut up."

IN THE MORNING PEOPLE CAME WITH PROFANE REQUESTS. "OKAY, in *Some Like It Hot,*" said a pensive young Irishman who smelled like a horse, "you know, on the set of *Some Like It Hot,* was there anything between Marilyn and Jack Lemmon, you know, romantically?" He was on the blue couch and she was on the chartreuse, from which she always received. She and her perfumed apartment made him feel shabby with his frayed corduroy cuffs and dirty work boots. She could see that he was embarrassed by the intensity with which he needed the answer to this question.

"What line of work are you in?" she asked, leaning forward discreetly.

"I drive a carriage around Central Park. For tourists," he mumbled.

"Oh! I love those horses. They are part of the *good* New York."

The Irishman looked even less at his ease.

"About your question. I'm afraid I don't know the answer."

"But how could that be?"

"Because I was Her in body, not mind."

"No!"

"I know, doesn't that suck? It would have been so much more meaningful if I'd gotten the whole thing." Until now Hazel had been glad of not getting the mind. Participating in the Irishman's thoughts, she felt bereft.

"You poor dear," he said.

"I'll be all right."

"You sure now, darling?"

"Yeah, sure."

"You're a bit of a sham, aren't you?" he said with great tenderness.

"Mm." Hazel gazed at the man, her eyes bright with tears. The man went away intoxicated with pity for the poor woman who had only been the shell of Marilyn Monroe. Without knowing it, this was what he had wanted to feel. The feeling put him in mind of the rhythmic overwhelm of a midnight mass in County Clare by the sea. He hadn't felt so deeply since leaving Ireland. In the elevator going down, he wept.

Next came a fifteen-year-old girl with dark freckles from Bensonhurst who chain-smoked mentholated cigarettes. Hazel didn't normally allow smoking in her apartment, but she sensed something brutal had been done to this child.

"Like, what happened with you and Bobby Kennedy and Jack Kennedy?"

"Could you be more specific?"

"I was reading this thing where it said they killed you. You were somewhere in L.A. and you knew too much and you sort of nodded out on heroin and then Bobby flew out in a helicopter and Peter Lawford came in and gave you a lethal injection and the Kennedys murdered you. Is that true?"

"No. I OD'd. I was by myself. I might have been saved if somebody was around, but nobody was around."

"Well then, tell me this then. Did those guys fuck you? Oh—I'm sorry, ma'am. I mean, did you sleep with those guys, Bobby and Jack?"

"What's your name, sweetheart?"

"Kathy."

"Kathy, there are things in a woman's life that are private and personal. Even if you like someone and trust someone, you don't always tell that person everything, do you know what I mean?"

"I guess."

"Kathy, look at me." Hazel improvised as she went. "Look into my eyes. I won't tell you about my sex life, but look carefully and see if you find the answer you're seeking."

"Nah, that's all right, ma'am. I can never tell anything from people's eyes." The girl seemed not happy but modestly satisfied with this exchange. She smiled to herself, the rare smile that was not meant for a reply. She winced.

"Is there something inside your mouth?" Hazel asked.

Kathy opened her mouth, reached in, and pulled out a razor blade. "Except when I eat or sleep," Kathy said. "It's for the gang I'm in."

"Would you do me a favor? I don't ask for payment. Would you give me that thing?"

"I'm sorry, ma'am, I can't do that. I have to take public transportation back to where I'm from through a couple of different neighborhoods. Do you want some cigarettes? I have five cigarettes. Do you want them?"

"Thank you, Kathy."

"Thank you, Ms. Monroe."

WHEN IT HAPPENS, THE FIRST THING SHE NOTICES IS THE ALMOST
bottomless cleavage blooming darkly between the lapels of
her white frock. Then her hair gets lighter and grows two
inches per second; it comes out the hair holes in her head as
if it had been waiting all this time, a big dry wad of balled-up
bottle-blond hair packed inside her skull where her brain
should have been; the hair coming out looks a little like a
horror show—some decent, ethical guy turning into a were-
wolf. Then Hazel is able to sing, "I wanna be loved by you alo-
o-one, poo-poo, pee-doo." Then she sings it. Her voice is
swooning and breathless. Everyone in the movie theater
leans toward her. They want her: a pandemonium of desire in
the movie theater. They all make soft moaning sounds, including Dina. When Hazel turns into Marilyn, everyone else
turns into a dapper chorus of musical-comedy zombies.
Hazel looks fabulous and feels good, but weird good. She's
been singled out for the supreme gift of voluptuous beauty.
She won't smile because a smile is nearly always a plea for
something, and there's nothing she needs to plead for. She
doesn't need anything or anyone, and that makes her laugh.
She could laugh all night. That's a little scary: the terror of
her tiny abyss. And then suddenly, as far as Hazel is concerned, beauty equals fear. The fear shrinks her, literally. Her
breasts go back inside her body, as does all that blond hair.

She is all Hazel again, and dazed, as are the people around her. She tries to hold on to the feeling of being two people: both beautiful, both serene, both afraid, both loved.

———————

THE MUSICIAN MENTIONED BY DINA TRURO NEVER SHOWED, BUT one day Dina's fiancé, Jim, came on his lunch hour to sit for a spell on the blue seersucker couch. They chatted awhile. Jim was fifty, eight years older than Dina. She wanted kids, was maybe too old to bear them, but Jim didn't want any anyway—already had some. That was what kept them from getting married. They were in purgatory.

"What are you here for?" Hazel eventually said from the chartreuse couch. It came out harsher than she had intended.

Jim was a hard, gray, pockmarked, middle-aged man. He was not born to the world Dina and Hazel had inhabited all their lives. He had muscled his way in. "You've got to talk some sense into Dina."

"What should I say to her?"

"She's on this thing about you."

"What?"

"She won't shut up about you. You're like Lao-tzu or something. Little aphorisms from Hazel, that's all that comes out of Dina's mouth. It's like when I'm with Dina I want to talk to Dina and who I'm really talking to is you, when I'm talking to her."

"So you're jealous."

"God, I hate that. Listen to what I'm saying, not what you think I'm saying." Jim had on a black coat. He was big and square, looming in the feminine living room. The couch was like a toy couch under him. His big, dark, loud self blotted out this piece of pale blue children's furniture. It was impressive.

"I'm sorry. What do you want me to do?"

"Tell her you're not God."

"And how should I bring that up? 'Oh, by the way, Dina, I just thought you'd like to know I'm not God.' "

Jim laughed once, the laugh like a bullet leaving a gun. He stood up and told Hazel, as he was walking toward her, that she'd figure out just what to do. Before she had time to get up he bent over her and kissed her softly on the mouth, lingering for a moment. It was a gentle kiss, a real kiss. It made her shudder.

———————

HAZEL'S LIFE WAS TERRIBLY FULL. HER WORK HOURS WERE GET-ting longer, and truth to tell, she found it harder to fit in time and energy for Dina. Insofar as Hazel continued to be two people, you might say that she had a built-in best friend, and

so if she saw Dina less, she did not immediately feel the pang
of missing her friend.

This was tough on Dina. She noticed Hazel's shift in behavior right away. As far as she was concerned, she didn't
really have her friend anymore. Her friend had graduated to
a higher plane: that's what she thought Hazel thought. In
fact, the place where Hazel's pangs were at their sharpest was
in the breast of Dina Truro. You get used to all the little comforts of someone who is in your life on a regular basis: her
smell, for instance; the shape of the little area of made-up
skin between her eye and her eyebrow. You don't even realize
how passionately they complete your days. So Dina threw
herself harder at Jim, which you might think he'd have en-
joyed, but without knowing it, she let slip a good amount of
unfocused anger at him: his skin was too rough, he was
coarse, all the complaints came down to his coarseness,
which is to say, his lack of being Hazel. So, by more or less
complying with Jim's wishes, Hazel was creating a more difficult love life for Jim.

It was late summer—hot, smelly, relentless summer in
New York City—all the death signs of summer, and none of
the life signs. Jim made Dina sumptuous dinners at night, the
way Hazel had sometimes used to do. He waited on her. He
plied her with wine, softened her up. She sat in his dining
room all happy, more or less, all giddy, anyway, while he toiled

in his hot kitchen, cooking up doubts. Late at night when Dina was half-canned on wine and loving attention, Jim burst through the double doors of his kitchen, singing, "Oh Trudy," singing, "Oh Trudy, Trudy, Trudy," and in his strong arms, big fancy platters of doubts.

So while Hazel Hess carried on her love affair with life, these doubts about her were being ingested by Dina, and not just that. The doubts worked their way through the inside of the very group of friends whose support was vital to the project of this period of Hazel's life.

So what was going on behind Hazel's back was also going on, in a sense, inside Hazel. It was going on, in a sense, in the largely uncontrollable place inside her that housed the Hazel that everyone else perceived her to be.

————————

ONE MORNING HAZEL WOKE UP AND MISSED DINA VERY MUCH. She called her and invited her for lunch. When Dina arrived she was cool and wary. They sat across from one another in silence, on the couches. Hazel always on the chartreuse couch. More of a loveseat. Trudy never sat on the chartreuse and Hazel never on the blue. Maybe Hazel should have gotten up off the couch, let someone else have the couch for once in her life.

"Hazel, I'm realizing I don't have a thing to say to you."

Hazel was dumb.

"Hazel, are we even friends anymore?"

"What do you mean? How could you say that?" Hazel asked, but she knew how.

"Maybe you should get out of the house more," Dina said.

"What?"

"I don't know."

"Why did you say that? What does that have to do with anything? Trudy, say more. Say what you're thinking."

"I don't know what I'm talking about. I don't want to talk to you. I don't feel like having lunch with you today."

Dina left. That was it. That was their visit. It was a three-minute visit.

Breaking up, if that's what you call it, with your best friend, is not like breaking up with your husband. For long stretches you convince yourself it's fine. You're *gently* devastated. It's the kind of devastation that doesn't seem to take a chunk out of your life. Rather, it's immediately part of your life. Blends right in. Strange but familiar. You can't believe it's happening, but it's happening, and it's happened before, but you're not sure when. You're looking at it a lot, you're nodding, yes, this old thing. Even as you're being devastated you're also already recovering. You're setting out, tireless traveler. It's way bigger than you, but you're holding it, on your skinny, brittle legs you're carrying it along, and while carrying you're sniffing, touching, tasting, testing, sampling all the moods your devastation has to offer. And it turns out you've sort of trained yourself for this kind of thing, because nobody but the most seasoned observer notices how badly you're hobbled by this experience that is so awful, that is so much deeper than humiliation.

Hazel did continue to see Dina at night when she was asleep. In her vivid dreams, she and Dina took frequent walks in the country, arm in arm. They saw things the real Dina and Hazel rarely saw: blue sky, green trees, red and yellow flowers, birds, rainbows.

"What kind of bird is that, Hazel?"

"I don't know, I've never seen such a bird."

"How about that one?"

"Don't know."

SHE CARRIED ON WITH HER WORK, WHICH WAS TO HAVE THE MOST meaningful conversation you could have with a stranger who came to your house, or something. Not easy work when your friends don't nourish you and Dina is gone. And the people who came in lately had the Lawford question a lot—did he kill her? Or did she have sex with Don Murray during the filming of *Bus Stop*? Or did she have sex with Joseph L.

Mankiewicz during *All About Eve*? Did she have sex with Robert Mitchum in *The River of No Return*? Did Clark Gable have halitosis in *The Misfits,* his last movie ever? That would be sad! And how many guys total did she have sex with in her life, and who was the best? She wasn't exactly phoning it in, but she was lifting the pinkie a lot more during this period of her work. If people came in shallow, she didn't go deep with them.

A mother walked in with her little boy. They had AIDS. This was seven in the evening on a Friday, and Hazel was exhausted. Polish immigrants. The dad of the family had been a heroin addict, died, but not before raping his six-year-old son. What do you say to these people? They had pale, falling-out hair. Skinny, sweaty, discolored. Hazel thought, "Will they leave a stain on my couch?" How could she go on thinking she was helping *anyone*? They didn't speak English, held themselves on her couch as if they were sorry to impose.

"Mrs. Klenewicz?" Hazel said. The woman's face brightened. Her son was too young and beleaguered to summon a concept of the contorted systems of delayed gratification he would have needed to experience hope: the kid's life was all bad; he just sat there. "Mrs. Klenewicz, do you see any crutches in here? Do you see crutches hanging from the robin's-egg walls of my apartment? Is there one crutch anywhere in here? This is not Lourdes, Mrs. Klenewicz. I'm not even religious. I'm not a Christian." The woman could sense by the tone that something was not right. "Christ!" Hazel shouted. Mrs. Klenewicz jumped back, startled, and Hazel made a cutting motion across her own throat, which she meant to mean "I am not Him" but that ended up meaning something much worse. "Nobody gets cured here of anything. I don't cure. This evening, Mrs. Klenewicz"—and even now Mrs. Klenewicz leaned forward with interest upon hearing her own name—"this evening I will not be solving any world plagues. I will not be ridding human nature of the disgusting, vile thing that it is."

"Vee aur sau-ry," Mrs. Klenewicz said. "Vee aur va-ree sau-ry to distoorb you. Hay-cell."

————

THERE WAS A KIND OF RECONCILIATION, NOT LONG AFTER WHICH Dina came over with some of the others, to go to the movies. Jim was there. He had an agenda for the day, which he perceived as merciful—you know, cruel to be kind.

They sprawled in her apartment, these handsome and well-groomed people sitting around her apartment like slobs. Jim took the chartreuse loveseat. He spread his knees wide and debased the seat. He held his head high and opened his eyes wide and defiant, like the chief of the bad rebel junta. Hazel stood uncertain in her own home. She was a small and thin woman. She hadn't had a hair appointment in a long time, and she was shaggy. She fluttered around her home in her shaggy hair like a starling in a storm. Dina was there, not to protect her friend Hazel. Dina had got a seat, looking helpless and satisfied. A few of the other boyfriends and husbands were there, dark, unshaven, looming. This was a man's day now.

"So let's go to the movies," Jim said.

Up Fifth Avenue they went again. Winter was in suddenly this year. One thing Hazel had done recently was to give away most of her clothes. She didn't have that smart red coat anymore. She shivered up Fifth and across Fifty-seventh. She wasn't drifting this year as she had been last. She was being carried along by this ravenous pack. Jim stated his agenda in that same red theater. "You're looking worn, Hazel. We think you need another rejuvenating movie transformation." You know what it's like when your friends have gotten together out of sympathy and plotted some degradation for you. Hazel reacted with a severe cramp in her midsection: a little sad starling bent forward, slightly.

The Manchurian Candidate was playing, and they challenged her to become Angela Lansbury. "I don't want to become Angela Lansbury, that's disgusting. I'd rather be Sinatra," she said, as if she were saying, "I'd rather be dead."

"So, be Sinatra," Jim said. "Be the evil Chinese guy, for all that it matters, know what I mean, Hazel?"

"I'm going to look for the precise seat I was in last time," she said, letting them humiliate her.

"That would prove it was the seat, not you."

The theater was not full, but they all sat in one row off to the side and somehow Hazel got the seat by the wall. Way over there, she wasn't even going to enjoy the movie, for Christ's sake.

Of course nothing "happened" that day, to Hazel or anyone. She quit the conversation business and found a job as CEO of a new, feisty little all-natural skin-care concern. She went shopping for new clothes, which she needed anyway since her wardrobe was kind of outdated. Dina was her friend but no longer her best friend. It took her years to develop a new best friend—a woman outside the old circle whom she met in a grocery store. There are only so many best friends you can go through in a life.

At first, when she thought of the Marilyn episode, she thought of it as one extended delusion; sure, maybe somebody got something out of it, but for her it wasn't worth it, it was very disconcerting, that was the truth about being Marilyn, she felt. Later Hazel recognized, with a sense of loss, what had been good about it. She thought of Marilyn's fleshy arms. She wanted to have clung to that good, soft torso a little longer. She wished she hadn't let her go.

Rose in the House

A family is seated at the dinner table. The mother mentions that she's been thinking about having her mother move in with them:

DAD: We can't afford that right now. We've got the kids, the cars . . . we've got to look at our retirement . . .
SON: Dad? Grandma could have my room. Okay?

—TV advertisement for financial services

"OH, GREAT, WHAT'S THAT SMELL?" SAID RONNY'S FATHER, Frank Selwyn, walking through the door of his own house on a Friday afternoon that happened to be the first day of summer.

"What smell?" said Sylvia, Ronny's mother, and she wasn't just saying it. She really didn't smell anything, partly because of her sinuses.

"I smell it all the time now."

"Since when?"

He wanted to say, "Since your mother moved in with us on Wednesday," which would have been true, but there are certain things a person knows not to say, even after that person has been hoodwinked into feeling magnanimous for allowing his mother-in-law to move in when it was not really his allowance to make in the first place; especially then. "Since a little while," Frank said.

"What's the smell?" Sylvia said.

"A rotting smell, stinking up the house. Possibly vomit."

"I don't smell anything," she said.

"I don't smell anything," said Ronny, wandering down the stairs into the small entrance hallway of their brownstone in lower Manhattan. He was the only child, a boy deep into the thirteenth year of his life whose bugged and skittish eyes inside an oblong face made him look as if he had just discovered introspection and found it alarming.

"You people don't smell that?"

"Don't smell it."

"Nope, Dad."

"There's no way you don't smell that. A rotten egg. A cherry bomb. A fart, son."

"Frank."

"Dad, did you just fart?"

"No gaseous by-product at this particular time."

Frank looked like someone's stern disciplinarian father but was in fact an amiable goofball fitted out with a father-shaped head. Ronny was amused now by a kind of comic dignity he saw in his father.

"Hey, Nanna Rose!" he called up the stairs to his newly arrived grandmother. "Your son-in-law just farted!"

"No!" Frank Selwyn grabbed his son's arm and hauled him into the living room. "That kind of talk is just for family."

"What's Nanna Rose?"

"I mean you, your mother, and me. I don't talk that way outside the three of us."

Ronny, a twelve-year-old boy in the body of a ten-year-old, was disturbed by this harsh reprimand. "What's with the weird reprimand?" he mumbled. He looked at his father's short golden hair and big round head; he appeared comical still, but it was now the kind of comedy that was also a kind of ugliness. And there was his mother standing on the other side of the room with her dark curls and a stupid, helpless expression on her face. He wished he were not an exact, fifty-fifty mix of these two people physically, and even more so, mentally. For in truth, introspection was his new full-time pursuit. In the last year he had gone from a casual, unexamined *boredom* with his parents to an active fear and resentment of them. He now felt that the entire purpose of parenthood was to steal the world from the child. Before he could think, or even speak, his parents had been at him relentlessly with their attitudes and assumptions and their personal styles, so that by the time he could develop his own consciousness it had been developed for him. Unbeknownst to him and without his consent, they'd pulled the old switcheroo: they took away everything and replaced it with the tawdry miniature of everything. This was an outrage and spur to a delicious mental privacy.

————

SOMETHING WAS THE MATTER WITH RONNY'S GRANDMOTHER, Rose Cornbluth. She was weak, she was thin, she liked her hand held while crossing the street. She seemed to lack the energy to boss anyone around in her usual fashion. Her daughter and son-in-law had noticed the change enough to move her into their own house, but beyond that they did their best to ignore it.

The night of the incident of the smell was Rose's third night in the Selwyn household. She had spent the first two nights on the fold-out couch in the living room. At dinner Frank still felt confused about his behavior in that incident. He was angry still. Without knowing why, he didn't want this lady sleeping in his living room. "We've got to resolve the sleeping arrangements," he said, trying to be cheerful.

"What's to resolve? Is it not resolved? Is there something unresolved?" Sylvia asked. She was having an acute sinus headache that required a lot of concentration. The sinus-adenoid area of Sylvia's body sometimes absorbed some of Sylvia's attentions and anxieties that had their true origins elsewhere.

"Well," Frank said.

There were three bedrooms upstairs. One was the master bedroom, one was Ronny's bedroom, and one was Sylvia's office, from which she ran a small agency for photographers and illustrators. Downstairs were the kitchen, the dining room, the living room, the laundry room. One bathroom downstairs, two upstairs. The function of each room had behind it the force of architectural destiny, with the exception of Sylvia's office. None of the Selwyns was going to say a thing about Sylvia's office. Rose Cornbluth did, and this despite some scary fights the two of them had had, love-breaking things, all those times they'd socked it to each other deep.

But Rose had her reasons now for pushing. "What about your office?"

"No," Sylvia said, fingertips gently to forehead.

"Out of the question," Frank said.

"How dare you?" Sylvia said to Rose.

"How dare I? Is that a question you want me to answer?"

"Mom, do we have to go over this? My autonomy from you? Et cetera?"

"No, but just as a footnote, if your autonomy is always going to be *from* someone, then it'll never really be autonomy, my point being why would you want autonomy from your mother?"

"Mom—"

"Rose—"

"Okay, so forget Sylvia's office." Rose hadn't wanted Sylvia's office anyway. She knew where she would end up.

"The question remains," Frank said. "Where are we going to put you?"

"Where are you going to put me? Where are you going to put me? I think what you're saying here tonight is you don't want me in your house."

Frank and Sylvia laughed.

"No, seriously," Rose said, "I can't be in the living room, obviously I can't be in the kitchen or dining room. Sylvia doesn't want me in her office—"

"Mom—"

"—which is fine. I'm sure nobody wants me in the master bedroom." Amused smirks all around. Rose, with a Yiddish-inflected Sherlock Holmesian finality: "This leaves—what?— young Ronald's room?" At this she put her hand on her grandson's shoulder. He cringed inwardly. He liked his grand-mother fine, but on the other hand she was a wrinkled old hag more in-your-face than his parents.

"You're gonna kick Ronny out of his room?" Frank said.

"I wouldn't dream of it."

"Oh no, Rose, that's not a good idea."

"What's not a good idea?"

"It's just not. Let's not even discuss it."

"Discuss what?"

"I'm sorry, but it's not decent for an old lady and a pre-pubescent boy to be sleeping in the same room in this day and age," Frank said.

Ronny felt an instant deep revulsion toward this utter-ance of his father's. There was something dirty about it. It had to do with the word "prepubescent." He felt as if some private thing had been exposed and violated. "Dad," he said, and stopped. He couldn't speak without participating in his father's truly icky degradation of him.

Frank knew what he had done to his son and regretted it. That regret was piled on top of the other injustice he had done Ronny this evening for no good reason. "I don't know what to do here," he said.

"Ronny, do you mind if I'm in your room?"

With only pure retaliation in mind Ronny said, "No, it's cool," and now he, too, was regretful.

"So, have we settled something here?" Rose asked.

Sylvia said, "Oy, my sinuses," and everyone laughed but the boy.

———————

AFTER DINNER RONNY AND HIS FATHER MOVED THE FOLD-OUT couch up the stairs, and Frank threw his back out and went to bed. Sylvia followed him holding to her forehead a blue plastic harlequin mask filled with some gelatinous substance that was good for her sinuses.

Ronny's narrow bed was situated in one corner of the room, and the couch, which folded out into a double bed, had been placed in the opposite corner. The positions of Ronny's desk and bureau had been adjusted to accommodate the new piece of furniture and the person who would be using it. There was plenty of floor space left in the room, but Ronny felt profoundly out of place in his most private dwelling. It had been the unique area of the world occupied only by him. It was as if his grandmother had just moved into his head. In fact, she had: he couldn't stop thinking of her. His thoughts would not be free of her for as long as she lived in his room. Would she remain in his room until she died? She was seventy-eight now. What if she lived to be one hundred?

Rose, having gone to the bathroom, returned in heavy green flannel pajamas, though it was ninety degrees outside. Ronny thought she looked cold even so. She eased herself down onto her bed as if she were in pain. "Go back into the bathroom," he wanted to say. He couldn't sleep in his underwear anymore! He wandered around his room, touching furniture, kicking a shoe, a Nerf ball, an ancient cookie from his youth.

"Sit down, you're making me nervous," she said. He glared at her. "All right, pace," she said. "There's something I need to tell you."

"You don't have to tell me anything."

"Shush. I'll talk, you listen. Sitting down would also be polite, but never mind." She paused. "I know you're not one hundred percent happy to have me in here, but I chose you and I'll tell you why. First you have to understand that my friends are gone. I mean really gone, forever, which you probably can't understand."

"If you know I won't understand, then don't tell me."

"Yes, I see. Point taken. So they're all dead, Ronald. That leaves me frightened. It's a little late for me to be seeking out new friends. My relations with your parents are complicated at best, as you have seen. You, I don't know. You're twelve— that's a major drawback. And then there's the way you're staring at me over there; is it the pajamas? Anyhow, I have had a hunch about you for several years. I suspect a spiritual kinship between us. What I'm trying to say here is, I'm old and I need someone."

This was a lot worse than he had dreaded it would be. Here was a lady who had to be the all-time world guiltmaster, breathing down his neck.

"Sit down, Ronald."

He sat. He was not being polite, he was being defeated.

"My friend, you've done an admirably decent thing by allowing your old grandmother to stay with you. I would like to repay you in the only way that I can at this time in my life: through the sharing of knowledge. Ronny darling, I'm going to lift up my shirt now."

"Nanna, what the hell are you doing?" Her shirt was already up around her ribs. Her soft belly was more than half covered with something dark red and craggy. There were small patches of smooth, pale grandma skin to be seen. She was showing him the red stuff, and when he saw it, he did what he would have done upon seeing a beautiful genius painting that no one had ever told him about: he looked away. He spent nearly a minute trying to think of everything he knew, first to compare it all to the new thing, and then, a futile attempt at working in reverse, to view each thing in the world mentally one last time before it was all changed by this red.

He looked at her again. She had put her shirt back down. "Mycosis fungoides," she said. "It's part of my lymphoma, which is a vicious kind of cancer. The worst."

"How come nobody told me this?"

"Nobody knows, except me, my physician, the entire oncology staff at the hospital, and my insurance company."

"Mom and Dad?"

"Nope."

"I'm telling them right now."

"Sit down! You are not allowed to tell them. They'll figure it out soon enough. They don't want to know yet."

"How do you know?"

"Trust me."

"Maybe you don't want them to know and you're just pretending it's them."

She raised an eyebrow. "Oh? And why would I do that?"

"I don't know. I'm not Sigmund Freud."

"All right, kid. Let's go to sleep now."

"What makes you think I wanted to know?"

"Ronald, are you sorry I told you?"

"Are you gonna die?"

With her hand, Rose shooed that question away from her head. She lay down slowly. "Turn off the light," she said.

Ronny turned off the light and got under his covers fully clothed. There, he changed into some old pajamas that were unfamiliar and too small.

Suddenly he felt a magical new feeling. It was indifference.

————————

THERE WAS ONE SECOND BETWEEN THE TIME RONNY WOKE UP and the time when he remembered about his new roommate. Then he saw her and practically said aloud, "Just die, lady. Die right now, why waste everyone's time?" because she was in the way of his new mental life. He was trying to start from scratch, mentally, and how could a person do that with a shriveled, pushy Jewish lady in his room?

Then he began laughing at something remarkable. Here it was, his first independent thought ever: he wanted her dead. How fascinating! This was it, this was the true dawning of his own mind. He spent a half hour lying in bed wanting his grandmother to die in various ways. There was a kind of platonic zeal here. He got up and nudged her shoulder.

"Ouch."

"Nanna Rose?"

"What do you want?"

"So are you gonna die?"

"Shut up. Weirdo."

"Come on. Death. Let's talk about it."

"Weird person."

"Don't say 'weird.' 'Weird' is not a Nanna word."

"I got it from you. You say it all the time."

"Do not."

"This is weird, that's weird. It's because of you that I've begun to view certain things as weird."

"Really?" He was easily flattered. Sure, this woman was a big, unpleasant digression, but on the other hand, maybe digression was the Fifth Avenue of a rich inner life. His friends no longer were interesting to him. Besides, they didn't like him anymore. So as long as Nanna Rose was going to be a regular pain in the ass in his life, he maybe could get some use out of her as someone for knocking ideas off of. "Are you gonna die?" he tried again.

"Would you stop it? You're gonna make me sick."

"That raises an interesting point. Did you throw up?"

Rose was lying immobile on the fold-out couch, an agile mouth attached to a worn-out old body. "You are referring to your father's remarks about the bad smell in the house?"

"How did you know about that?"

"I was at the top of the staircase listening."

"Dad's got a good nose. Me and Mom always say what a good nose Dad has."

"That's exactly what I'm saying about your father."

"What?"

"They don't want to know I'm sick. 'What's with the smell?' 'What smell?' 'That smell.' 'This smell?' 'Which smell?' 'This smell.' 'That smell?' The entire point of that spiel, including your father's anger, was to talk about the smell instead of the thing that was making the smell, which is me dying."

"Cancer makes you puke?"

"No, the medicine they give me for the cancer makes me puke."

Now they heard the yelling. The two other inhabitants of the house—whom they were discussing but whom they had both forgotten—spent all of Saturday morning in a loud argument. Rose suggested to Ronny that they leave the house quickly and eat an outdoor brunch in the park on this warm and sunny day in June. He didn't have anything else to do, so what the hell.

———

IT WAS NEARLY NOON WHEN ROSE GRASPED RONNY'S HAND A little frantically and he helped her across the street into Washington Square Park, which is a big rectangular park that you couldn't quite get lost in. Tall, thin black men, mostly Jamaican, stood around at all the major entrances in not-so-wonderful clothes. "Hello, Mrs.," said one of the men.

"Hello, Troop," Rose said. Ronny was amazed. "This is my grandson."

"Uh-huh." Troop now looked uncomfortable and backed up a few steps.

"His name is Ronald Selwyn. Ronald, shake hands with this man."

"Lady, you're nice and everything, but I don't want to be knowing your grandson. I got a bad feeling about standing around chatting with you and your grandson, you know what I'm saying?"

"Stop it, mister. Just because you're a criminal doesn't mean you don't have to have manners."

Troop, who was twenty-five years old, took quick, ambling steps in several directions while looking from side to side. "Yeah, okay, uh, Ronny. Nice to meet you." He shook Ronny's hand. "Whoa, strong handshake," he said without conviction.

"You look out for my grandson, Troop."

"Now there's a shitty idea."

"Shush your mouth."

"Are we gonna do business today, ma'am, or you just stopped by to make introductions?"

"Give me twenty dollars' worth of marijuana, please." Rose reached into her small red-and-white leather purse as if she were going to pull out money to pay for strawberry preserves.

"This is unbelievable," Troop said, his eyes still moving quickly from side to side.

"This *is* unbelievable," Ronny said.

Rose handed Troop a twenty-dollar bill, and he handed her a one-inch by two-inch Ziploc bag bulging with marijuana. Troop seemed genuinely frustrated and upset. He walked away from the old lady and her grandson, left the park, and headed purposefully down Waverly Place. Several times he made a gesture as if throwing something down hard onto the sidewalk.

Rose guided Ronny to a bench in the park. She went through her purse like a sweet old lady again and this time brought forth a soft, curvy mahogany pipe the length of her index finger. She loaded it with a clingy little green bud of marijuana. She withdrew a lighter from the red-and-white purse.

"We're gonna get arrested!" Ronny said, knowing it was a lame-o loser comment inadequate to any of the last eighteen hours' events, but he had to start somewhere, commentwise, and work his way in. Rose looked at him in dismay, as if she were having second thoughts about bringing someone this uptight on this particular adventure. In that way she was behaving in the prescribed manner of the pot mentor, and Ronny was doing his part as the initiate.

She lit the pipe, inhaled, held it like a true teenager, and exhaled. "It's for the nausea that comes with the chemo, by the way."

"I'm not a moron."

"And for you I suppose you could be using it to advance your personal consideration of topics such as Death, and so on."

She passed him the pipe. He'd never smoked before and didn't want to now, but he'd made a dweeb of himself in front of an eighty-year-old with that line about getting arrested, which made him somehow beholden to her. He inhaled and coughed. It was painful. She laughed and patted him on the back. That too is standard and universal; the older roommate teases the younger; far and wide the attitudes and sequences are observed. She took one more puff and said, "I'm cool now, man," and presided over several more hits off the pipe for Ronny, each followed by a coughing fit.

And now time gets all funny. Time's winged chariot embarks on a series of dizzying loop-dee-loops. Marijuana time—like time spent in the company of a special loved one—separates itself out from all other time and becomes continuous with itself. Thus it is unclear if Ronny truly got off on the pot that first day, or on the second or third or fifteenth day. They smoked on the same bench on each of a succession of nearly identical sunny and hot days, which didn't help anyone to differentiate.

And every one of their conversations was extremely important, though in what way was not always clear, and each one was memorable but impossible to remember, just as the actual sensation of physical pain is impossible to remember, and for entire afternoons at a time Ronny forgot to resent his grandmother.

"Could I get cancer from this?" he asked, one day during the week or on the weekend, in the early afternoon, during the month of June or July.

She tried to stare him down, but he said, "Don't patronize me with that stare," and giggled.

"Drug companies don't want to research cannabis because they wouldn't be able to patent it. Not to mention all these nice young black men carrying light weapons here in the park already seem to be doing a brisk business."

"Is it going to stunt my growth and give me brain damage?"

"There are worse things than stunted growth and brain damage. But hey, kiddo, you don't have to smoke pot with your old grandmother. Of course I'll be insulted, I'll feel abandoned and lonely, but that's perfectly fine because I'll be dead soon enough."

"God, Nanna, you are an asshole sometimes."

"Listen to who's calling his grandmother an asshole. If you're worried about brain damage, don't smoke."

"Too late, I'm already addicted."

Grandmother and grandson fell silent for long stretches. Their little bench faced the southern part of the island of Manhattan. They were subject to loud reggae music played on the portable stereos of young white students at New York

University. A group of these boys, informally known as trusta-farians, often gathered in the area near the bench to keep a small, tight leather beanbag aloft with their feet and knees. A few of them wore their hair in the same shape as the hair of some Jamaican marijuana salesmen, which is to say their hair resembled big wads of sticky marijuana.

The long gaps in conversation reminded Ronny of a the-ory he had inadvertently developed as a young child that two people who knew each other well should have almost no need for talking. There was that, and also the theory that a man and a woman who really loved each other would have sex all the time. The second theory he had been able to refute through the extensive porno-magazine research he conducted both with his friends and on his own (though admittedly in this area he still had much ado to know himself). As to the first theory, he was baffled that it was so undercorroborated by his parents' marriage. The only things they should have been say-ing were very practical-type instructions, such as "Also get a head of red-leaf lettuce." But these people were yammering at each other all the livelong day. He figured that was because of him. The joint venture of a pregnancy, of having a kid, of nam-ing the kid, of taking the kid shopping, of keeping the kid extra extra happy required almost constant negotiations that extended way beyond the actual kid himself. I mean, sure, he had ruined his parents' marriage—so what else was new? But there was more here than he was putting his finger on. Now, on the bench, he was hoping to go further into this topic of love and its requirements than he had ever gone before, but the sun was so hot, and there was drift.

"Why are my parents yelling all the time lately?" he asked his grandmother.

"They're screaming about my cancer. Particularly your mother. She doesn't know I have cancer, so she screams at your father about something else. It helps to scream when you don't know something terrible. Of course once you know the terrible thing you're not allowed to scream anymore. This is partly why I'm not telling them. Earnest screaming is dé-classé. These days if a person starts screaming in earnest, that's considered bad manners."

Ronny found his grandmother to be full of it. Nevertheless, she was entertaining.

"Also," Rose said, "married couples need an argument to keep things regular."

The word "regular" reminded him of doody, and he giggled for a short time. Very old people and very young people have in common a preoccupation with their bowels, so the both of them giggled for a minute, maybe, on that bench, one afternoon in July or possibly June.

"But seriously, their marriage, do you think it'sa gonna last?"

"Did you just say 'it'sa gonna last'?"

"I didn't mean to, it just came out that way. Answer the question."

"Oh come on, Ronald."

"Where are we going?"

"Don't worry, it'sa gonna last. Of course their marriage is not as solid as mine and your grandpa Herbert's . . ."

"That didn't seem so great. You two seemed, you know, like a couple of old people who were tired of each other. Like, 'I can't believe I'm still with *him* after all these years' or whatever. When you were with Grandpa you looked like you were expecting something better."

"That's the failure of your own imagination."

"I know what I saw."

"Your parents are doing fine, but a modern marriage can't be as good as an old, traditional one."

"Remind me why again."

"Weapons of mass destruction. Mustard gas, the H-bomb, electronic information creeping over the surface of the planet like a flesh-eating virus. Nothing means anything anymore. This is also why so many people are taking Prozac, by the way."

"Or smoking pot."

"Touché."

ONE FRIDAY NIGHT IN THE MIDDLE OF AUGUST FRANK SELWYN
had a bout of coughing at the dinner table. "Has anyone noticed how much more dust there is in the house than ever before?" He was trying to be wry and comical, but he was
talking too loud, as if all the fighting with Sylvia had dulled
his sensitivity to volume. "What is with this dust? I find huge
wads of dust on the floor. My stereo components are covered
in dust the day after I dust them. Is there some decaying or-
ganic matter somewhere in the house?"

Rose kicked Ronny under the table and rolled her mari-
juana-reddened eyeballs as if to say, "See what I'm saying?" As
for Sylvia, she was on the verge of tears without knowing why.

"I don't know," Frank went on. "All this dust, it's a sign of
doom, which began very recently, I might add."

"Say what you mean, Frank. You mean it began when my
mother arrived."

"Oh boy, are you instigating," Frank said.

"Face it, that's what you're talking about, and we all know
it. It's too late to complain. Why are you complaining?"

"I was under the impression that I was making morbidly
amusing dinner chat, as is my wont. I love your mother. Who's
complaining?"

"Know thyself, Frank. The unexamined life, Frank."

"If I wanted to complain, I'd be talking about the financial
duress she's putting us under at a time when, as you well know,

I'm juggling moneys to the ultimate benefit of our family. It's risky now, is all, because of the sheer amount of moneys being juggled. But I was talking about dust, not your mother."

"And it's a good thing she's not here," Rose said, "because now we can feel free to talk about her. Ronny, is there anything you would like to say on the topic of Rose, before she shows up and ruins this great opportunity?"

"She's a pothead."

"Don't you make fun of me," Sylvia said to Frank, though it was not he who was making fun of her.

"Don't you make fun of me!" Frank said to Sylvia.

Sylvia was officially crying now, and she left the dinner table. "I guess I'm not hungry," Ronny mumbled, and went up to his room.

"Get back here, fella," Frank said, still trying somehow for joviality. Ronny kept going. Frank left the table without looking at Rose. Rose had no appetite because of the cancer. She followed Ronny up to the room. The dinner table remained alone, full of food.

———

By now Rose had great difficulty walking. the journey up the stairs exhausted her. When she opened the door to the bedroom Ronny said, "Do you have to always be in my room when I'm in it?"

This remark cut Rose. Ronny was so used to her presence he barely noticed he'd said anything. She sat down on her bed feeling that this particular bout of unhappiness among all the ones she'd had in her life was the one she would carry with her straight into death. Ronny lay on his bed already thinking of other things.

They stayed in their positions for a while, and then Rose went for her purse, the red-and-white one, the last purse she'd ever own. She took out the pot and the pipe. She'd been using the pot more and more. By now it wasn't for the nausea.

"You're gonna smoke that in here?" She ignored him and held her lighter up to the pipe. "Holy shit, are you out of your fucking mind?"

"Listen, Ronald. I may smoke marijuana, but I'm still an unreconstructed seventy-eight-year-old person and it upsets me when I hear you using that language."

"Mom and Dad will kill us."

"Please."

"Nanna, you're a selfish old lady."

"I'm selfish?" She lit the pipe and took a drag.

"Fuck."

He got a glare from Rose.

"Well I can say 'fuck' if you're gonna stink up my room with pot and get me in serious trouble with Mom and Dad beyond anything in the entire history of punishment."

This was the second time Ronny had referred to *my room.* "Oh. So this is your room."

"Yes. It is. And you're a welcome guest in it, but you can't smoke that in here."

"That's bullshit."

"So you're allowed to curse."

"When something is utter bullshit, yes. It's your room and I'm a welcome guest. Well, you're different from what I thought. You're like them. I should never have taken you into my confidence. I'll be packing my things and leaving tomorrow."

"Jesus, Nanna. You're crazy. You're senile." He looked at her carefully to see if she was kidding. Lately he expected his grandmother not to be a stupid typical absurd old lady, and sometimes she disappointed him. "Knock it off," he said. "Like I need this on top of Mom and Dad acting like idiots. At least deal with me as a human being enough to tell me how I offended you. I'm not a moron, you know. I understand stuff when it's explained to me."

"Too late. You blew it. I'm leaving." Rose shut off the light and carried her transistor radio to bed with her. There she found a reggae show on a local college radio station, and she rocked herself to sleep to the simple, trancy one-drop music. Ronny, meanwhile, stood fully clothed in the middle of his room in the dark for half an hour.

IT HAD BEEN A ROUGH SUMMER, AND ROSE WAS IN A LOT OF PAIN. None of this was how it was supposed to go, but this was how it was going. The morning after her falling-out with Ronny, a Saturday, she made an attempt to walk to the park. She opened the front door and was greeted by a wall of hot air. She stood leaning in the doorway for a moment feeling every machine that generated heat in the city: every car, every subway, every jackhammer and bandsaw, every mainframe computer, every generator and air conditioner. People were living all wrong now. She wished to have lived in the old New York—men, women, and children strolling the sidewalks in small, stately groups, entering their cozy homes, eating meals together, reading aloud from great books by the fireplace, each conversing with each, no one excluded, burying their dead in Washington Square.

She hadn't the oomph to make it to the park. She retreated into the house and dragged a chair toward the window in the dining room that overlooked Waverly Place. It gave her some small satisfaction to watch the maneuverings of a particular middle-aged Jamaican marijuana salesman whom she had had dealings with. He was small, eloquent, dark-skinned, always a little drunk on cheap beer, ridiculously cautious in his transactions. She became absorbed in watching him direct a customer to place a ten-dollar bill firmly in a crack on the sidewalk and pick up a certain empty pack of cigarettes lying by the wheel of a parked car.

Suddenly Ronny was standing above her in the dining room. He said, "So."

She looked him over from head to toe. "You have crappy posture."

"Oh, I have crappy posture." It was easy for him to see how much her body ached.

"You're sweating like a pig."

"Oh, I'm sweating like a pig."

"When it's hot out, let me teach you a lesson, snot-nose. Good posture. Walk slowly, good posture, serene. Breathe. Kindness to others. In through the nose, out through the nose and mouth. Posture undergirding this."

"Where do you pick these things up?"

"At my age, you know. You, on the other hand, are ignorant."

"I notice you haven't left town."

"Shut up. Someone has to stick around and relieve you of your ignorance. Nuggets of wisdom. McNuggets of wisdom, snot-nose. Where would you be without me? Sweating like a pig with terrible posture your whole life."

At first Ronny had thought that the dying of such a lively conversational partner would deepen his own life in a sort of

fun way, without a price, because dying was a scary enter-
tainment that didn't necessarily have death at the end of it.
But now he could see it coming. He understood how much
her death would kill him. In other words, he was experiencing
the true beginning of introspection in his life.

Rose was wearing white cotton athletic socks without
shoes. Her feet were swollen. "Nanna, I have an idea."

"I doubt it."

"Foot reflexology."

"This is what type of idea?"

"I massage your feet, and each part of your feet is attached by neurons to another part of your body that's not
your feet. It could provide relief to your whole system."

"First he wants me out of his room, now he's providing relief to my whole system. Mother Teresa and his relief effort."

"What do you think?"

"I think it's disgusting."

"Let me try it."

"I'm wondering, does the word 'schlemiel' mean anything
to you?"

Ronny pulled over a dining room chair and sat down.
"Give me one of your feet."

"Get away from me."

"Foot, please."

"Pervert."

"Left foot."

"Stop it."

"Oh, come on."

"Where are we going?"

He reached down and gently took hold of her left foot. Rose was putting up a fierce, final struggle, which Ronny hardly noticed.

"I'm not a helpless old coot. You mustn't treat me this way."

"Rose! Cut it out!"

Rose turned her face up toward Ronny's. She appeared frightened and obedient, as if he were her scolding father. Her leg went slack. He placed her foot in his lap and rolled up her pants leg to the knee. There was almost no grandma skin to be seen—just the dark red, cooling lava-looking stuff. He became so absorbed in his ministrations that he didn't see the shaking of her shoulders, or the tears on her cheeks, now that she had capitulated.

They lapsed into just another one of their silences. Rose cried without making a sound. Ronny pressed the tips of his fingers softly into the bottoms of her feet while looking around at the dining room, which he was trying to memorize, now for a different reason from before. He had recently made a vow to himself never to forget what it was like to be twelve years old, though he knew such an effort would not come in handy for anything whatsoever. It—twelveness—was just something he needed to carry with him, a powerless talisman, a complete, sad world coexisting with but hardly touching whatever sequence of worlds he would be required to inhabit as he grew older and further away from these moments.

Though no one had recently smoked pot or vomited, Sylvia ambled down the stairs and, as she turned the corner into the dining room, said, "What's that smell?" She looked puzzled when she saw Rose's foot in Ronny's lap. Then she saw the grotesque, reddish skin on her mother's lower leg. She didn't know exactly what it was, but it took her less than a moment to figure out what it meant. "What is that?"

"Cancer."

She stood in the doorway of the dining room for a while, then she leaned up the stairs and called Frank down so he could look at the cancer. He came into the room and saw. "It's cancer," Sylvia said to him. "How could we not have known?"

Frank and Sylvia hugged each other and stared at Ronny's hand, which was skimming lightly along the diseased surface of his grandmother's leg.

"I suppose I'll die quickly now," said Rose, and she did.

A Car

Dreamlike images appear: a girl in a white
dress on a swing, malevolent clowns holding a
gigantic key . . .

GIRL, VOICE-OVER: It was like some kind of bad
dream. By the time Dad was finished, I was scared
to death of buying a car. . . . It would be obvi-
ous this was my first time. . . .But there were
no hassles. Even over the price.

—TV advertisement for a car

OUR DAUGHTER'S BODY IS A REPROACH TO US. SHE HAS RE-cently turned into a little monster of physical fitness and moral rectitude. Which doesn't mean that I don't know there are shifts in a family, and that no one is ever prepared for them. I remember, for example, the entire year when I was ironic. Maybe I hit upon irony because it is the thing that terrifies me most. Irony is like an evil twin that clubs you over the head, gags you, throws you down the basement stairs, and takes your place at the breakfast table with your family. And it says exactly what you would say, only instead of saying, for instance, "I love you," it says, " 'I love you.' " I was ironic for a year because that was the period during which I was in-fatuated with a certain woman in my office. I would like to point out that even during that year, I was loyal to my wife and daughter almost down to the tiniest scruple. It must have been awful for them.

Still, my infatuation ended, and so did my irony. Our fam-ily mended and moved on. It's different with Susie, our daughter, who is sixteen years old. We're afraid her current behavior is not merely a mood but a temperament.

The three of us have had a tradition of eating breakfast together in our pajamas, but lately Jane and I teeter down the stairs stiff and weary on our skinny legs, rubbing the crust out of our eyes, and Susie is already in some absurd yoga position on the floor of the breakfast nook. One morning we showed up and Susie was kneeling on the clean, bare linoleum floor in her little exercise getup, thighs smooth as plastic. Without ceasing to kneel, she lay back with her legs tucked under her. The back of her head and the nape of her neck were touching the floor. We could see her ribs and the outline of her hard little abdomen under her cotton jersey. She inhaled deeply and said, "You two are like a furnace of foul odors." She said it with such good humor that we didn't know how to take it. The whole thing was very odd. From her position on the floor, all lean and contorted, she had this power over us. Jane and I looked at one another, and I could see that it was a bad day for Jane. We turned around and walked slowly up the stairs, no doubt with terrible posture, and we got back into bed and we fell asleep.

She runs ten miles, she swims three miles, she rides her bicycle forty miles, she does her homework, she works at a tanning salon after school and saves her money, she goes out with her nice friends and has a good time engaging in moderate activities. She's going to buy a new car. I want to say to her, "Susie, get a fake ID and have a few drinks. Buy a quart bottle of Wild Turkey and get sick. Borrow my car without asking. Skip school. Smoke pot. Have an affair with a forty-year-old alcoholic woman with a ring in her nose." But Susie runs fifteen miles. She runs thirty miles.

————————

MY WIFE'S BODY FITS MY OWN SO NICELY, OUR UNGAINLY, SAGGY bodies, as we lie in bed holding each other and talking. It's a bit of solace against this stinking world. The other night we were discussing Susie's impending purchase of a new car. Jane said, "Can't you take her aside for just fifteen minutes and tell her what kind of a crazy circus she's going to encounter in car sales?" We were lying on our backs, angled slightly to face one another. Her head was resting on my arm, and our bodies were in gentle contact all the way down to our ankles. The lights were off, but I could see Jane's face as it was illuminated by the street lamps our town government had put up and by the small lantern we have in our front yard, both of which are on timers that turn them on an hour after sunset and off an hour before sunrise. Jane's face is not beautiful, but there is nobody's face I would rather look at. Show me the most gorgeous twenty-eight-year-old model for eyeliner or moisturizing creme—my heart might race for a couple of seconds, but don't make me face her for an hour. Familiarity is better than beauty. The extra grooves in Jane's skin, the puffiness around the eyes, the small amount of flesh that has accumulated below her jawline during the twenty years of my having looked at her steadily: these things are a life's work. Jane and I own each other's skin.

"Yes, that's good," I said. "Circus. That's just it. It *is* a circus. But how am I gonna tell her? You know how she is."

"Please. Don't tell me about how she is. I'm her mother. It's worse for the mother. With the father I don't think there's the same humiliation." I could see the echo of the word "humiliation" in the muscles of her face the instant before she smiled in that pained way. "Humiliation" has a particular meaning for us. Rather, it has a particular meaning for me that Jane is aware of. She doesn't know the details of the single event in my life that makes the word resound at the very core of my being—namely, the ending of my infatuation with the young woman—but she understands. This seems to be the gift of women: to know the feeling of an event without knowing the event. Thus Jane can say, "Oh, I saw the most wonderful movie on public television the other night," and I'll say, "What was it called?" and she'll say, "I can't remember," and I'll say, "Who was it by?" and she'll say, "I don't know, I think it was Australian," and I'll say, "What was it about?" et cetera. (In this regard, by the way, our daughter, Susie, is more like a man.)

"Okay," I said, "now tell me what you mean by circus."

"You know, they're a bunch of clowns, car dealers. They'll deceive her with illusion and falsehood. They're famous for it. The whole enterprise is just going to be another defeat for our family. Could you go with her maybe?"

"You mean accompany her while she shops for the car? First of all, she probably won't let me. Second of all, it's a dreadful prospect, spending a goal-oriented day with that supercilious little American girl."

Jane laughed. "Oh, for Christ's sake, we've got to help her."

A car went by on the street in front of our house, and we both watched the crucifix-shaped shadow of our window frame move from one side of our bedroom ceiling to the other.

"My arm is asleep," I said, and tried unsuccessfully to wiggle it out from under her heavy head.

"It's funny that you say, 'My arm is asleep.' What you really mean is that your arm, as the result of a trauma, has fallen unconscious. Your arm has fainted. It's been overtaxed. Your arm's getting older, dear."

We laughed. Jane didn't move her head, and I didn't move my arm. We fell asleep.

———

I MADE A POINT OF GETTING UP EARLY, SHOWERING AND DEODOR-izing, shaving, and putting on a fresh, crisp shirt and pants before going down to breakfast. As I approached the door to the kitchen I saw Susie's two tall, clean, golden legs sticking up side by side from behind the table in the breakfast nook, toes pointed. "Morning, sweetheart. I'm all clean and not smelly."

"Look, this is the candle position, Dad. Can you touch your toes?" Her entire weight was balanced on her shoulders and neck and the back of her blond head. I don't know where she got her coloring from, since Jane and I are brunettes. She exhaled and rolled forward one vertebra at a time. When her legs were flat out in front of her she continued to move forward until her fingers were holding the bottoms of her feet and her face was between her knees.

"Susie, are you going to start your car hunt today? I thought we should just talk over your strategy on buying this car."

She didn't answer. Her breathing was steady and slow. It was clear that these idle greetings and questions of her father's were an annoying distraction.

After she had held that same position for a couple of minutes, she unfolded herself and stood up. She went to the cupboard and got a glass, which she held under our refrigerator's automatic ice dispenser, and then she took the carton of orange juice out of the fridge and poured some into the glass. "We should stop buying this stuff," she said. "*Consumer Reports* rated a couple of the new electric juicers really high.

I think we ought to invest in one. Most of the nutrients are lost in the concentrating and rehydrating process, not to mention the flavor."

"What do you do, casually flip through *Consumer Reports* in your spare time? Most girls your age are languishing in their rooms listening to Janis Ian over and over, reading *Seventeen* magazine."

"Most girls my age don't read. They also don't save their money or spend it wisely." My daughter talks this way, like Ben Franklin or something.

"So about the car," I said.

"The Japanese cars seem good," she said. "There's that new American car company that seems to have a lot of integrity. I'm looking at the area between compact and midsize. Gotta have passenger-side airbag. Gotta have antilock brakes. I'm thinking four-wheel drive for winter safety, but I'm not sure the terrain in this area demands it."

"You don't know where you'll be going to college," I said.

"Good point, Dad. Excellent point," she said thoughtfully.

It's pretty rare that she finds something I say worthy of consideration. I could feel myself blush. I had momentum, so I said, "I just want you to be careful because even though you may know a lot about the cars, the car dealers are tricky and deceitful. A car dealership is like, you know, a circus. You go in there, they throw a lot of jargon at you. They say 'reclining bucket seats' and 'V-6 engine' and 'ergonomic design' and 'hard-body steel construction' with big smiles on their faces."

"Dad, give me a little credit for knowing something. Also you're exaggerating the evil in human nature as usual."

"No. You know what? You give *me* a little credit. I'm not paranoid. I have actual experience with car dealers. I've bought cars. I even once knew a car dealer. If you do this all on your own, you're gonna get hurt."

She was silent for a moment. "It sounds like you relish the idea of me getting hurt," she said. "Excuse me, I'm going for a bike ride."

As she walked out the back door I called after her, "I do not relish the idea of you getting hurt."

———

I OFTEN HAVE THIS SENSATION AFTER TALKING TO SUSIE OR JANE that I've left out the most important thing. I can never put my finger on what it is, but I feel that if I were to say it, even once in one conversation, it would make us a winning family instead of the other.

———

"SHE RESENTED MY INPUT," I SAID TO JANE THAT NIGHT.

"Don't say 'input,' " she said. " 'Input' " is like 'reclining bucket seats.' "

"You're right," I said. " 'Input' is a dirty word." We were lying in bed again. Inertia is the epitome of our marriage. I don't mean that we don't change or that we're frightened of progress. I mean that our last moments of consciousness each night, when we talk and lie together, amount to a dark nest of quiet truth amid all the racket. Our conversations are the opposite of a car.

Jane smiled and snuggled against my soft, hairy shoulder. "What did you say to her?" she asked.

"I said the thing about car dealers being clowns."

"But what was the point? What were you hoping to persuade her to do?"

"Let me come along and protect her." As soon as I said this I pictured Susie's body, which is like a coat of armor, and I realized how absurd a thing it was for me to protect her, and so did Jane, and we had a good laugh.

"So I guess she turned you down."

"I guess so."

"Are we just going to let her go through with this by herself?"

I sighed. We were silent for a moment, and I could hear the alarm clock ticking on the night table on Jane's side of the bed.

"I mean what are we going to do with her?" Jane said.

"Pack her off to boarding school?"

"I think really she needs the opposite of boarding school."

"What's the opposite of boarding school?"

"Maybe she could climb in bed and sleep with us the way she used to?"

"Maybe we could accidentally push her down the stairs."

Jane gasped and rushed to put her forefinger to her mouth and say, "Shhh," as if suddenly Susie could hear our whispers from down the hall. But I saw that smile breaking out behind her finger.

THE FOLLOWING DAY WAS A SATURDAY. AT EIGHT-THIRTY A.M. ON my way to the bathroom I saw that the thermometer outside our bedroom window indicated sixty-five degrees. In anticipation of Susie's subtly perfumed limbs at breakfast that morning I lost all hope and went back to bed for an hour and a half. Jane and I were feeling so embattled that when I finally did get up, we agreed that I would scout out the breakfast nook. If *she* were still there, I was to grab a box of cereal, some milk, a couple of spoons and bowls, mumble something about "your mother's menopause," and retreat to the bedroom.

"Dad," she said, before I had caught sight of her, "let's go, get a move on, shake a leg, I want to have a car all picked out by five o'clock this afternoon." She had evidently finished with her yoga. She was wearing a new pair of fancy jeans, an off-white short-sleeve silk blouse, a delicate gold necklace, and elegant brown pumps: a car-hunting outfit.

"What?" I said. "You want me to go with you?"

"Of course I do, Dad. How would I be able to do this without you?" There it was: Susie's evil twin.

I showered. I put on a polo shirt, khaki pants—the Dad outfit.

As we were walking out the door Susie threw on a blue blazer, put a Walkman in her pocket, stuck the tiny speakers in her ears, and proceeded to listen to music that only she could hear.

"You gonna wear that thing when we talk to the salesmen?"

"What do you think I am?" she said, louder than she needed to.

———————

THE FIRST PLACE WE WENT WAS TO THE SHOWROOM OF THE AMERican car with integrity. We walked in. No one approached us. All the walls were made of glass. The lighting was subdued. The air smelled processed. The cars were shiny and resting gently on the gray carpet. I felt as if we were in a fancy restaurant that had cars instead of food. I became nauseated. What did she need a car for? She was sixteen, she could ride her bike. I prepared myself to forbid her to buy a car.

Susie marched us over to one of the sales offices. When I caught a glimpse of the salesman sitting behind his desk I put my hands over my face. In the few moments my face remained covered by my hands I gave up on Susie, I gave up on her altogether. Then I turned so that my back was to the salesman, dreading that he had seen my face, and I asked Susie to step away from his office for a moment.

Very quickly and monotonously I said, "I've decided to let you handle this by yourself. I think this car company *is* different and they won't take advantage of you. This will be a good experience too, for you to buy a car on your own. If you can do this, you'll be ready for adulthood."

"What? Excuse me, Dad, but this is very weird."

"I've thought it over, this is what I want you to do. Here are the keys to my car. I'll take the bus home."

"Thought it over? It seems like you, like, are freaking out on the spur of the moment. You said you were gonna buy the car with me."

"You didn't really want me to."

"Yes." Her face was red. She looked confused. It was all I could do to walk and not run for the door of the showroom.

The salesman, you see, was the husband of that young woman who had caused me to be ironic with my family for an entire year seven years ago. I had known way back that the guy was a car salesman, but it must have slipped my mind. Not only had his wife worked in my office; she had been my secretary. I cannot put into words how beautiful she was. I had thought that any life with her in it would be better than what I had, no matter how high the price.

I had wanted to fire her, but there were no grounds. For a year I practiced self-restraint. Then, one warm Friday in spring, when everyone else in the company had gone home, she wore a sleeveless blouse into my office to water the plants, and I got down on my knees. She was standing above me, and I took her hand and told her I loved her, and I asked her if she would go away with me the following weekend. She ran out of the office and never came back.

For several months after that, I came home from work, ate dinner, and went to bed; on the weekends I slept as much as possible and rarely left the house. I did not tell Jane what had happened, but my irony was gone and I'm sure she understood, in that way she understands without knowing. What she did was remarkable. She spent the time in bed with me. If I lay in bed until noon on a Saturday, she lay in bed until noon. If I went to sleep at eight o'clock on a work night, she climbed in next to me and held me in her warm arms. It must have been tough on nine-year-old Susie, her two parents hiding in the bedroom, cohabitating in their defeat.

———————

JANE WAS NOT AT HOME WHEN I ARRIVED. I DIDN'T KNOW WHAT TO do with myself. I sat at the kitchen table. I saw ahead of me an afternoon of sitting and waiting, and I was afraid.

At this point I had the following thought: "What would Susie do?" The answer was that she would run ten or fifteen miles and then go for a thirty-mile swim. So I actually went up to our bedroom and found a pair of sweatpants and a T-shirt and put them on. On the way down the stairs I felt hopeful. Then, in the driveway, I felt stupid. I was in my pajamas, practically. Then Jane came up the driveway in the station wagon.

She got out of the car and laughed. "Say it isn't so!" She was referring to my jogging attire.

As a kind of preemptive strike, I scrutinized her outfit. She never dresses well. She had on an old pink T-shirt with a worn, frilly hem. It was too small for her. Her jeans were baggy, and her tennis shoes, which she had worn to play tennis about twice, were dirty and frayed. Her graying brown hair was stuck up on top of her head with a random assortment of bobby pins and barrettes.

"What happened? Did you get kicked off the car-hunting team?"

I nodded.

"Ooh, you look so cute in your getup." She came over smiling and grabbed my shoulders and kissed me all over the face, making with each kiss an enhanced, artificial kissing noise—"mwa"—as if we were a brand-new couple in our twenties.

"Frankly, you don't look so great at the moment yourself," I said, before it dawned on me that she was not being ironic.

Her face looked pained, and then calm. "So it really smarts that Susie wouldn't let you shop for the car with her, eh?"

"Yeah, that's right," I said, "I guess it really does smart."

Now she squinted, which meant she knew there was a discrepancy between what had happened and what was being said. "Why don't you come inside," she said, "and we'll split a beer while we wait for her to come."

There was such assurance in the way she said that, and in the way she hooked my arm with hers and steered us toward the front door, that I was afraid of her. Surely when Susie got home my lie about getting kicked off the car team would be found out. And if I sat across the kitchen table from Jane just waiting for Susie to come home, it was conceivable that all my lies would be found out. "I feel disgusting. I'm going to take a shower," I said.

"Do whatever you want."

AS I WAS DRESSING I LOOKED OUT OUR BEDROOM WINDOW AND saw Susie coming up the driveway in a brand-new economy-size hatchback from the American car company. I ran downstairs and out into the driveway. Susie got out of the car. Her face was flushed. I gave her a big hug. "I'm sorry, honey," I whispered before Jane caught up with me.

"Dad, it's fine. It worked out for the best. You'll never believe what happened. Mom," she said to Jane, who was strolling toward us, "you'll never believe what happened."

"What happened?"

Sweat was pouring from my armpits onto my freshly laundered polo shirt.

"So we're in the car taking a test drive, just me and the salesman, right?"

Jane and I nodded eagerly. Here was this beautiful new car in our driveway that Susie had purchased all by herself. Jane was infected by the car and by Susie's radiance. The two of them made their mouths into these big alarming smiles.

"So we're on the highway, right? And I'm driving? Well, this guy puts his hand on my knee. The car salesman does. For real." Jane stopped smiling. "And then he starts asking me things and saying things to me. I can't even tell you what they were because I'd be too embarrassed. But he said like five separate gross things to me. I had no idea what to say to him, so I didn't say anything, I just concentrated on getting back to the lot as fast as I could, but I also didn't want to get a ticket or anything.

"And then, check this out. Mom, Dad, when we get back to the lot I have this brilliant idea. Dad, remember how I had that Walkman in the pocket of my blazer that you were giving me a hard time about? Well, I jump out of the car and show him the Walkman, and I, like press one of the buttons like it had been on the whole time, and I say, 'Look, mister, I just recorded everything you said to me in that car, and that is totally sexual harassment. Not to mention I'm a minor.' So you know what I made him do? I made him sell me the car for fifteen hundred dollars below list price. I got the Achilles for six and a quarter! Is that awesome or what?"

Susie laughed with sheer joy and jumped up and down, and she wanted her parents to jump up and down with her, but we were too old and out of shape, and her story was actually pretty depressing.

Even though I thought it might still emerge that I had abandoned Susie at the door of the salesman's office, among other things, I feigned happiness, as Jane seemed to be doing, and I said I'd take everyone out for a nice celebration dinner, only we'd have to go in Jane's or Susie's car because mine was still parked outside the car dealership.

Susie went up to her room, and Jane and I sat down across from each other at the dreaded table in the breakfast nook.

"What do you make of this?" Jane asked.

I had my hand over my mouth. I shook my head.

"Did you meet this fellow, the pervert?"

I shook my head again.

"You didn't see him."

"I saw him."

"But you didn't meet him."

"Right."

"You didn't really get kicked off the car-hunting team, did you? You resigned, didn't you?"

I thought this was it. I saw everything collapsing. "How did you know?"

"Please," she said. "I understand."

"You do?"

"Well, no," she said. "I really don't understand. I believe there's something . . ." She didn't finish the sentence. She stood up and walked to the window that overlooks our driveway and stared down at Susie's new car. Then she came back to the table. "Whatever else happened, it's clear to me that Susie's story is false," she said. "Let's get ready for dinner."

I tried to take Jane's hand and walk up the stairs with her, but she pulled her hand away and went up by herself.

When I got to the top of the stairs I heard water running in the bathroom down the hall. Susie was taking a shower, though she had taken one just before we left to buy the car. I have since verified that Susie did indeed pay six and a quarter for the car, but, like Jane, I don't think it happened the way Susie said it did. Behind the sound of the shower was another sound, a funny noise. I walked down the hall and stood outside the bathroom door and I realized what the noise was. It was Susie sobbing. That means she's not as good a liar as her father is. Surely this fact alone constitutes a victory for our family.

How I Greet My Daughter

A middle-aged woman is just waking up in bed
while her daughter is already in the kitchen
making coffee:

SONG: She finished school and moved back home.
Will you be close now that she's all grown?

—TV advertisement for coffee

SOMEBODY HAS GOT TO GET THIS DOWN ON PAPER, AND IT'S not going to be my daughter because she's an idiot. It will have to be me, her mother.

She showed up at my house—i.e., my life—one morning and said, "Mom, I know you hate me but this is my first divorce, and I don't know where else to go."

"I don't hate you, but I do want you to go away," I said. I liked the optimism of "my first divorce." She's not without charm, my daughter. Her face looked terrible. I'm all too susceptible to the terrible faces daughters show their mothers. Jenny's face just then reminded me I was not alone in the world. How delightful to be alone in the world! As opposed to how I live, which is I haul that face from one day to the next.

I invited her in for a glass of water. It could have been worse. I could have invited her in for coffee in a mug with the word "Mom" on it. I don't drink coffee because I hate the feeling of coffee, which is like a visitor in your body, someone with greasy skin who is ill at ease.

"I'm all sorry and everything about your divorce although I say good riddance to the creep and you'll get over him and so on, but first and foremost is that you can't stay here for more than, say, an hour." (An hour—too long!)

"Why?"

"Because I already breast-fed you and drove you to and from ballet class seven hundred times."

"I'm staying here," she said.

"I'll call the police."

"Are you aware that everything you've said to me my whole life has been some variation on good-bye?"

This is exactly why I don't want anyone in my house, particularly her. People sitting around reading each other like books.

"I want to tell you how my marriage fell apart," she said, apropos of nothing. She's never been good at conversation. Nobody I know has ever been good at it.

"Absolutely not."

"Why?" she asked.

"Would you want me to tell you how my marriage to your father fell apart?"

"That's different."

"Everything is the same as everything else," I said.

"It's different because you're the mother and I'm the daughter."

"No, darling," I said. "I'm the nothing, and your father, also the nothing, married me, and a while later I gave birth to you, and consequently you, too, are the nothing."

She started to cry. She was sitting at my kitchen table. Have I mentioned she's enormous? I am this tiny little speck in my brown bathrobe, and she is a gigantic blond thing with thick limbs that shoot out of her body and come at you from unexpected angles. She cries every time she comes to my house.

I left the room and went into one of the other rooms. The house has a good number of rooms, and I have strolled them at night hugging myself, which is—need I say?—better than having a visitor.

I looked out the window—something I never do. Beyond this house there is very little that I know about anymore. There's a golf course across the street from me in this suburban town. I don't ever see the golf course, but all the short green grass is part of my world view. If my body is the Eastern Seaboard, then the golf course is the Great Plains of America. The swimming pool all the way at the other end of the golf course is California.

An hour later I went back into the kitchen. She was still crying. I told her, "This disruption is nothing short of brutal." I think she understands my dry wit, because she stopped crying then.

"Can I make you some lunch?" she said.

"Get out."

She looked through my kitchen cabinets and opened the door to my refrigerator and saw that it was empty. "Where are the keys to your car? I'll get some things."

"I'll get some things!" I shouted.

"You'll get them?"

"No."

"You're funny." Not only had she stopped crying, but she was cheerful, girlish.

"Where are the keys to your car?" she asked again.

"I don't have a car."

She saw the keys on the kitchen table and took them. "Back in half an hour."

"I won't let you back in the house."

"The keys to the house are right here on the key chain next to the car keys."

She left at noon and came back long after dark. "Met up with an old friend and had a drink," she said. "Hm. Wow."

"A drink, eh?"

"More or less."

"What did you buy at the grocery store?"

"Coffee."

"Get out."

"Nowhere to go."

"Go stay with your friend."

"He's not that kind of friend."

"Oh, I see, he's not that kind of friend. Get out of my house!" I stamped my foot and shook my fists.

"Here's why I'm not getting out." She walked right up to me in the kitchen. I was leaning back against the kitchen counter, and she is a freakish giant. She stood so close to me that I could see murder in her face. "Because," she continued, "you've ruined me for marriage. I'll never be happily married because of you. You raised me for a life of loneliness and paranoia."

"All right, then I'm leaving," I said. I ducked past her. By now it was ten P.M. I changed out of my bathrobe into some clothes. I hadn't been out of the house in a year and a half.

How shall I describe driving a car again? Everything was ninety degrees off from where it should have been. So there was this vertical surface—the earth—with a narrow, vertical line of asphalt—the road—going across it. I was trying to keep the car on the road. Below me the great, grassy expanse of golf course swept downward toward nothing at all.

In a hard parking lot, I got out of the car and the ground rushed up to greet me. Once my body was in full contact with the ground I didn't want to move, because it seemed if I stayed in one position I was less likely to fall off the ground. There were people nearby finding a variety of ways to show that they wished I was not there on the ground where they would have to look at me, and not run me over with their cars, and other inconveniences for them. They showed these things by, for example, not looking at me and not running me over.

I got up.

I went inside a small, brightly lit store where they had rows of refrigerators with transparent doors that you could look through to see all the food being kept cold. Normally a man brings the food to my house in a plain cardboard box, so I didn't recognize any of the food in the context of these refrigerators. I picked something out and microwaved it. I don't know how I knew how to microwave it. What I didn't know how to do, then, was eat it. I didn't know what it was. It was modeled on food a future society will use when shape and color and texture and presentation and taste are no longer concerns.

Keeping a low center of gravity, I conducted the car back to the house. I got out of the car and went into the dark house and got into bed with my clothes on. There was someone in my bed. It was nice to have someone in my bed without having to plan it or ask for it. I hugged the person. The person hugged me. Then I remembered it was Jenny, my daughter, and I tried to hit her with my fists, but she held me so tight I couldn't hit her. I was outraged, and the outrage took over my whole body as I had hoped no feeling would ever do again. The shaking of my body frightened me—I clung to my daughter in my outrage against her, just as she clung to me so I wouldn't hit her. My face was wet. Jenny was whispering something to me. I couldn't make out the words, but the sound of her whisper appeared as a thread, and I picked up the thread and held on to it and it led me into sleep.

In the morning I smelled coffee. I was alone in bed. She was up ahead of me. I went into the kitchen, and there she was, spilling out of my brown bathrobe. "Coffee, Mom?"

"What did you whisper to me last night?"

"I told you the story of how my marriage fell apart."

We both knew there could be only one consequence of the previous night's events for a mother and her grown daughter. Telling her to leave for the last time was merely the signal required by etiquette. "All right, Jenny," I said, the pitch of my voice sloping downward toward the foregone conclusion of this episode. "Now get out of my house."

"No, Mom," she said, and that is how my daughter came to live with me.

Bridesmaids

An interview with two young women who say they have been bridesmaids a total of nineteen times:

WOMAN #1: I get the dress first and I call Melissa in Texas.
WOMAN #2: Fuchsia?
WOMAN #1: Wait, I said. It has a hoop.

   —*TV advertisement for long-distance phone service*

Do you find it at all odd that we're on our nineteenth tour of duty as bridesmaids and not once has either of us been a maid of honor?" Katherine asked.

"Because they know we're best friends and they think the one they don't pick will feel insulted," Lydia said.

"Your relentless optimism," Katherine said. She was the taller one, the more vocal, the more forceful, the less shy. She had driven down to Los Altos from San Francisco late Saturday morning, picked up Lydia. They were on their way to the rehearsal dinner in Big Sur.

In her quiet way, Lydia always tried to resist this grim, knowing Katherine tone. The effort depressed her. "So why do you think Angela has been picked so many times? She's not exactly a raging beauty," Lydia said.

"Angela is slutty. Slutty is perfect for a maid of honor. It's like, she's not as beautiful as the bride so she won't show her up, but she's sexier than the bride, but that's okay because also she's sluttier than the bride, so the groom's relatives can

look at Angela and go, Well, he made the right choice because the maid of honor's a slut."

"Oh, maybe I should become a slut," Lydia said.

"No."

"I know, but just tell me why not again."

"Self-respect," Katherine said. "Furthermore"—and despite what Lydia perceived as Katherine's general pessimism,
she liked Katherine's use of bold rhetorical terms like "furthermore"—"Furthermore, being a slut means bringing total
strangers into your home, and who knows what the fuck
you're getting?" Lydia also liked Katherine's use of bold
rhetorical terms like "fuck." "What if you and some guy are
suddenly, like, naked, and he refuses to wear a condom and
you say no and he forces himself into you? Do you think that
kind of guy is so rare? No. And why?"

"Because men are dogs," the two said in unison.

This was one of the phrases Katherine and Lydia had
spoken a thousand times since they'd met in college, either
individually or, as they had taken to doing lately, in unison,
and with each new utterance, each phrase took on a new
layer of shared significance; they laughed, and each knew
roughly how much sadness the other's laughter contained,
because somewhere in the San Francisco Bay Area a not-
especially-nice group of boys was sitting around someone's
shabby living room drinking beer and, over loud music, calling *them* dogs—not all women but Katherine and Lydia—

sharing a different significance and a different kind of humor.

But Lydia liked to be upbeat. She said, "Well, you're not slutty but you are sexy, K. You're that skinny-girl-with-big-tits kind of sexy. Guys love that."

"Please."

"You are. I mean, in comparison, think of my breasts, if that's possible. And I'm not chubby but I read as chubby?" Lydia didn't want to put herself down now but felt she had to for Katherine's sake. She wouldn't do that anymore, after the wedding.

"How many guys have loved my body in the last year?" Katherine asked. "None. And in the year before that? One. And how long did he last? A month."

"This is your problem is your attitude," Lydia said.

" 'No you're the sexy one, no you're the sexy one, no you're the sexy one,' " Katherine said, mocking hundreds of conversations they had had over the years. Something really was bothering Katherine. "But seriously," she went on, working herself up into an intensely ambiguous tone of voice, "a lot of guys go for little breasts like yours. Your body is such a total little unit. If I were a guy I would take one look at your tight little body and I'd want to just stick it to you."

Lydia got a chill because for a moment she felt Katherine had sort of become the guy who was having that aggressive sexual thought.

Lydia was vigilant against such darkness. She worked out every day, she was advancing in her software job, she read good books and not trashy ones, she made sure she had plans with friends at least four nights a week. She even, in a perfunctory way, kept up with the horrors of politics and history—like the tragedy in Bosnia—if nothing else just not to sound like a moron in a conversation with any stranger she might happen to meet.

They continued south on the Pacific Coast Highway, which is mostly a two-lane road that runs like a hem along the edge of the continent. They passed artichoke farms and little beach towns and low-rent vacation spots. Soon they were up on the cliffs over the ocean. It was a sunny day and the water was high and frosty and beautiful and the low, flat, peach-colored clouds above the horizon were beautiful. Lydia was un-Californian in that she was not a Buddhist or a pantheist or a shaman or a mystic. Statistically, she knew it was extremely improbable that she was the center of the universe, and yet subjectively she knew that she was, and she also knew that it was healthier to think of herself that way so people wouldn't take advantage of her. Just now, being the hub and all, she felt it was impossible that everything around her could be so delightful to behold if she herself were not.

She rolled down the window of the car and took huge, refreshing inhalations of air. "Close the window, it's cold,"

Katherine said. Lydia closed the window and stretched her legs out in front of her and flexed the quadriceps and relaxed them and her body felt strong and rested. "Isn't this scenery heartbreaking?" she said.

"Yeah, heartbreaking."

"What's the matter with you?"

"I'm not up for this wedding. I'm grim about this wedding. I'm sick of weddings. Enough weddings already."

———

THE REHEARSAL DINNER WAS HELD IN BIG SUR ON THE TERRACE of a large restaurant built on a cliff overlooking the Pacific Ocean. There were twenty-nine guests. Lydia noticed the long, thick black beard worn by the only one of the grooms-men she had not met before, and then she noticed the broad shoulders, clear, dark eyes, rosy cheeks, and full lips of the bearded stranger. The core twenty-nine were lingering in the part of the proceedings during which people stand around on the terrace in small, awkward combinations—the bride's father with his first and second wives and the bride's older sister's husband, say, or Lydia with two grandmothers and the best man, or Katherine with the bride's fifteen-year-old step-brother. Lydia, despite her premeditated decision to branch out and be friendly and open and easy to talk to, really wished Katherine had not deserted her upon arriving at the restaurant. Katherine, for her part, was getting a small, dreary kick out of arousing the fifteen-year-old by talking nonstop about explicit sex scenes in movies she had gone to that year, while giving him occasional puffs on her cigarette.

Just before the appetizers were served Lydia managed to corner Katherine and mention this unusual beard she should keep her eye out for. Then the appetizers were served and people took their assigned places at the table. Lydia was one seat away from being diagonally across from the beard, and about eight seats away from Katherine, who was seated next to the groom's little brother and best man—a junior in college so much handsomer and more well-mannered than the groom. The sky was clear, and the air felt warm though slightly cool and carried a faint scent of eucalyptus, and the sun was close enough to the surface of the Pacific Ocean that a gaudy pink and orange and purple light filled the western half of the sky. Lydia felt now that she was fighting for her enjoyment of these gorgeous surroundings. On her left was a grandmother who could talk of nothing but her husband languishing in the hospital; on her right was the fifteen-year-old boy who, encouraged by Katherine and dizzy on nicotine and wine, periodically assaulted Lydia with innuendo, on the theory that all twenty-five-year-old women got a kick out of keeping young boys in a constant sexual delirium. Lydia preferred the very sad but interesting conversation of the old lady. She wanted to give old people more of a chance than most of her peers gave them, and she often discovered that it was well worth listening to their stories. "I'm learning here about the nuts and bolts of the suffering of people who are in their eighties," she thought. Hospital bills, Medicaid, Social Security, U.S. savings bonds, pensions, prostate, osteoporosis, Alzheimer's, bad circulation and swollen ankles, heart attacks, overall dwindling of tissue. These are the things it couldn't hurt to think about at Lydia's age, for reasons of both empathy and preparation. Some self-abnegating politeness prevented her from keeping her back turned away for the entire dinner from the boy who was too drunk and aroused to quit pestering her with his bland, warlike concept of sex, but for the most part she concentrated on the deeply unhappy grandmother of the groom. And she hated to dwell on this, but frankly this aged woman smelled heavily of talc, which was all right, and of a familiar but ultimately mysterious geriatric lotion of some kind, which was also fine except that it seemed to be concealing a smell that Lydia could conceptualize only as the smell of biological decay. Twice she caught the eye of the man with the red lips and rosy cheeks and beard, and he smiled at her warmly. And that was good because she was feeling cold.

Of the twenty-nine guests at the rehearsal dinner, fifteen gave toasts. First on his feet was the wonderful little brother. He had bought a dark blue suit for this moment. Someone had told him that he wanted his first adult suit to last, in

terms of quality of fabric and craftsmanship, as well as dura-
bility of style. It was a Wall Street pinstripe, and Lydia
couldn't have imagined anything more adorable. Here was a
young man most comfortable in athletic shorts and a netted
lacrosse shirt. Here was a graceful, delightfully proportioned,
animal-comfortable body, a happy body under the severe
cloth; just the way his thick wrist emerged from the sleeve,
widening out into his hand holding the wineglass as he said,
softly, "Well, Tommy is my brother and now Nancy is going to
be my sister, and that's so great because I've always wanted an
older sister." He looked at the couple, he smiled. (No way!
Could those be tears in his eyes?)

His toast was an ode to the kind of role models the groom
and bride were for him, and yes, he was crying a little bit, and
to Lydia, who was not one to go out of her way looking for
ironies, the irony here was what a decent human being this
best man was compared to his oafish and basically football-
watching older brother.

By the end of the twelfth toast the guests had been
seated in their chairs a total of four hours. During toast number thirteen, Lydia noticed that Katherine was standing over
the best man and speaking quietly to the top of his head. He
seemed not to notice. Then Katherine bent down and said
something directly into his ear. He tilted his head up and
chuckled lightly without taking his eyes off the bride's oldest

sister, who was giving the toast. Katherine slapped the wide shoulders of his suit. She was drunk. She had begun a rambling monologue, quieter than the bride's sister's toast but heard by the eight people nearest her. With fatherly, restraining hands, the best man patted Katherine's hands. She removed them from his shoulders and shut up, for a moment. She lightly swatted at him and whispered to him until, in the last remaining grandfather's speech, she grabbed the sleeve of his coat and held on. He shrugged out of the sleeve and was up out of his chair facing her in one unified motion. He chopped the air once, his hand in the shape of an axe, and his fine shirted arm came to rest an inch from Katherine's nose. He said something angry to Katherine—Lydia thought she heard the word "bitch," but she wasn't sure. He sat down. Katherine walked away from the table.

After the dinner, when people were dispersing to the prearranged cabins and suites that dotted the steep hills above the Pacific Coast Highway in Big Sur, Lydia had just worked up her nerve to say something to the man with the big black beard. In the restaurant parking lot, she looked at him tentatively, raised her eyebrows, raised, even, her hand to wave hello. He smiled broadly and said, "Hi!" And then Katherine came up behind Lydia talking fast. "Lyd, Lyd, I'm out of cigarettes, where do you get cigarettes, this is like a health town or something, they don't sell them here. Is there a bar where there are cigarettes? Maybe all the young people could go out drinking." The bearded man was already moving away toward an all-male evening with the other groomsmen. "Bye!" he said sympathetically, and Lydia said "Good-bye!" and Katherine said, "See you tomorrow," and Lydia was annoyed.

———————

"THERE'S SOMETHING WRONG WITH THIS ROOM," KATHERINE SAID to Lydia when she unlocked the door of the deluxe sleeping quarters they would be sharing. Now she was a hundred percent on Lydia's nerves. Opening the door to this huge, dark room long after sunset could have been almost a profound experience for Lydia had Katherine not insisted upon degrading the silence with her careless yammering. The warm, dry air of the room smelled gently of sea salt and roses, and through the enormous west-facing picture window Lydia could make out not so much the visual outline as the feeling of the dark, steep, green drop down to the water and the water's limitless and thrilling blackness. But Lydia found herself bound to this person who made a point of being irreverent toward all the little private ceremonies Lydia could give herself as a comforting trail of loving gifts leading to the big public ceremony at the heart of the weekend. Katherine turned on the lights.

Now Lydia tried to look out the window, but she could see only her reflection and Katherine's. Suddenly she knew what Katherine had meant when she said there was some-thing wrong with the room. "It's us," Katherine said aloud, and Lydia mouthed silently. "This is all so lovely, and what are we? Two trivial, horny girls in formal wear."

"But, Katherine, haven't you noticed? Most people aren't lovely," Lydia said before she knew what she was saying. She shuddered.

"I am a bony heterosexual woman with wide, childbear-ing hips whom no man will ever love."

Lydia changed into a T-shirt and sweatpants and walked to the huge black window. She pressed her face against it. It was cool. She raised up her arms and pressed as much of them as she could against the window.

Katherine paced the oriental rug in her long floral dress. "Did you see what an idiot I made of myself during the toasts?"

"What the hell *were* you doing?" Lydia cupped her hands around her eyes and tried to see what, if anything, was out-side their room.

"I wanted Cal to walk with me along the beach. What the hell was I doing?"

"Cal? That's his name? Oh my God."

"I couldn't believe him in that suit. I was staring at his neck. I wanted him to swim naked in the ocean. I couldn't stop myself."

"Don't worry, K. I saw how wonderful he was. Cal."

"I'm an idiot, idiot, idiot. Did you see him with that wine-glass?"

"He's adorable." Lydia peeled herself off the window and sat down on her twin bed. Katherine changed into an over-sized T-shirt and sat down on her bed facing Lydia. "You can try a different tack with him tomorrow," Lydia said.

"No I can't."

"So what? That's not what we're here for anyway."

"Yes it is. Speaking of which, I managed to pull aside Beard Man and tell him you wanted to meet him."

"Who asked you to do that? I didn't want you to do that." Lydia's heart raced.

"Listen, he said, 'Good, we'll talk tomorrow at the reception.' "

"He did?" Lydia was almost standing up.

"He seemed interested."

"Oh, Katherine!" She leapt forward and hugged her friend, and kissed her on the lips. Then she stood up and turned off the lights and they lay down, each on her own bed. Lydia's skin tingled. She was thinking of the quick kiss with Katherine, and she knew Katherine was thinking of it too. Lydia remembered one morning ten years ago when her parents came to breakfast whistling and smiling, and she knew they had just had sex. Now she felt a pleasant heat seeping from her pores out into the darkness. This was the physical

sensation of hope. The kiss was not so sexual as it was ro-
mantic, implying an intimacy that spread out beyond the two
of them to an easy give-and-take with the whole wide world.

───────────

NANCY, THE BRIDE, WAS JEWISH ON HER MOTHER'S SIDE AND
incorporated into the otherwise Unitarian wedding ceremony what Lydia thought of as a brilliant Jewish touch. On
the small platform that was the altar, she walked in a circle
around her groom seven times. This was something she
wanted to do for him: surround him, make an invisible force
field between him and the world. Lydia wanted that in her
own marriage; not the circling—the force field. She wanted
it around her. Since, of course, Nancy did not pass over the
head of the groom, there was a hole at the top of the cylin-
drical barrier, through which Lydia thought God could enter
the groom's brain in the form of marital thoughts.

Still, for all the fuss, there had to be one single miracu-
lous pinprick of time in which the man and woman were
transformed into the family. And then the wedding was done.

───────────

BEFORE THE HUNDRED AND SOME–ODD GUESTS WERE SEATED FOR
lunch at the big, fancy, standardized hotel in Monterey where
the wedding was held, Lydia found herself standing in a

threesome with Katherine and the man with the beard. He stood more than six feet tall. He wore a black tuxedo with white tie and cummerbund. It fit him perfectly. His cheeks were rosy, but he was no boy. His black beard was a foot long. "I admire the way you two are wearing your fuchsia bridesmaids' dresses," he said.

"You like these things?" Katherine said.

"I didn't say that. I just said you're wearing yours well. In fact I've been to a number of weddings now, and the one theme linking them all together is this ugliness of the bridesmaids' dresses. Maybe it's part of the tradition to insure that the bride will look great, in case there are some really pretty bridesmaids." He had the good sense not to say "like you two," but the inflection was there. Katherine and Lydia exchanged a meaningful glance whose meaning neither one could decipher. The conversation continued for a while. Lydia's face was so actively engaged in responding to everything the man said to Katherine and everything Katherine said back to him that Lydia didn't notice she herself said nothing.

When the five-piece wedding band laced into their first number the man turned his body toward Lydia, opened his arms, and asked her to dance. She was mortified. The band played a medium-tempo swing tune, and he didn't just dance modern style—separate, improvised. He held her and danced her. This man knew how to dance. Lydia didn't have to do much. She went where he gently directed her. Sometimes she was out at the ends of his arms, sometimes he pulled her close to his torso. She didn't know what to look at. She looked at the band, she wondered where Katherine was, she peered around for the bride and groom. When the song was over she was greatly relieved. He held her two hands in his. She knew he was looking into her eyes. She could not return the look. A slow song started. "One more," he said.

He pulled her toward him so that the entire length of her body was touching his. The top of her head almost came up to his chin. Her left cheek grazed the coarse animal hairs of the beard. He held her not aggressively but firmly. She had no idea what song this was. She couldn't hear the music. He managed—this is how good a dancer he was—to find the way that the fronts of their two mismatched bodies would fit snugly one into the other. This was all just so embarrassing for Lydia. She wanted to feel something sexual, but she couldn't, she couldn't. She decided to put her ear against his chest and close her eyes and try to listen for his heartbeat, which she would then try to use as a mantra to calm herself. It was acceptable for the girl to close her eyes in a slow dance, even if she wasn't the guy's girlfriend, but Lydia's were clenched, and anybody looking would think there was something wrong with her. She opened her eyes and saw Katherine, several yards away, swilling champagne, smoking, laughing with the bride and groom. It was amazing how unhappy a single dance could make a person.

The electric-organ player, a tall blond man, said, "And now, ladies and gentlemen, take your seats because it's TIME FOR THE APPETIZERS!"

Lydia sat next to Katherine at a table with all the other bridesmaids and couldn't eat. Katherine talked: "That Cal, he came right up to me after the ceremony and said, 'Sorry I was such a jerk last night. I was uptight because it's my brother's wedding and everything.' Can you believe that kid? But seriously, Lydia, he's just a kid, which I realized today, but he's going to make some girl very happy someday." She kept talking. Lydia listened, sort of, and made the motions of eating her appetizer. She had withdrawn into herself.

When the appetizers were cleared away the band started up again. Katherine was still talking. Lydia was having one sip of champagne a minute. She didn't like the taste. Here came the man with the beard, which was what Lydia was having one sip of champagne a minute for. All right, she was loose, she was loose. Here he came. He was coming to her table. Here he was. "Katherine," he said, "your turn."

"Oh, no, not me. Lydia's the dancer." (Thank you, K.)

"Katherine," he said, mock sternly. She stood up.

It was an up-tempo number, and he danced Katherine with the same authority, only she talked to him, and he talked back. Lydia kept going one sip a minute with the champagne. She thought she ought to look at something other than her best friend dancing with the man she had a crush on, but she couldn't turn away. Yes, he was a man. Lydia thought of herself and Katherine as girls, but this bearded person, who was their age, was neither a boy nor a guy. That was because his beard was an adult male beard. It was thick, not experimental or tentative. It was a part of his completeness. Not only that, but he extended himself out into the world, sexually, with the beard. They danced close to Lydia's table. She didn't look away. The band played a slow song that was a little faster than the slow song they had played while he and Lydia were dancing, and he whispered something into Katherine's ear, and she blushed, and after a moment she whispered something into his ear. He whispered something back right away.

The song ended. The man walked away. Katherine swept down upon the bridesmaids' table, scooped up her full champagne glass, drained it with her head thrown back so that Lydia could see what a long, pale, beautiful throat she had, and then Katherine said, "My God, he's like Rasputin!" more to herself than to Lydia, because if she had really been saying it to Lydia, what an inconsiderate thing it would have been to say, and off she went.

The entrées came and Katherine was gone, and so was the man. Lydia couldn't eat. She finished her glass of champagne and made herself go pay respects to the bride and groom and their parents and grandparents. "They must be off doing cocaine somewhere. Katherine must somehow have scored a Ziploc bag of cocaine in the city and she's been feeding herself from the bag for the entire weekend and sharing with everyone except me because she knows I'm a prude," Lydia thought. The same grandmother from the rehearsal dinner got ahold of Lydia's arm and pointed out all the handsome young single men for her to dance with. Each of this woman's smells had intensified since the evening before, and Lydia couldn't remember why she was supposed to be polite to old people. She wanted to say, "Hold the thought, lady, I have to go piss my guts out," but it came out, "Excuse me, I have to use the ladies' room."

In fact she didn't have to use the ladies' room. She walked toward the ladies' room. A freckled, red-haired woman in her mid-thirties whom Lydia didn't know was coming the other way. She made some kind of face at Lydia and muttered something. She was trying to tell Lydia something, but what did Lydia know? She didn't know anything. Sure, when she got within several feet of the ladies' room, a place she really didn't have to use, there was a feeling in the air; more of a sound, but for Lydia it was a feeling.

Had the lights grown dimmer? Had Lydia remembered to put her contact lenses in that morning? She splashed water on her face at the sink in the ladies' room. Somebody cried.

Sure, it was a wedding; doesn't someone always end up in the ladies' room crying? The person was in the middle stall. There was a lot of commotion in that stall. Lydia started to say, "Are you all right?" but she stopped at "A—." Somebody—it was Katherine—said, "A—" just when Lydia did, except she said "Aaaaaaaa." Lydia bent down to look under the door of the stall and stood up quickly because she had seen four shoes under there—a man's big black oxford, a woman's little fuchsia pump, a man's big black oxford, a woman's little fuchsia pump, all facing the back of the stall. Katherine's mouth was wide and the noises were coming fast. Lydia thought it would be more embarrassing for Katherine and the man with the beard if she, Lydia, were to leave now, so out of politeness she stayed. Could anyone's pleasure really be that intense? It sounded as if she were being slowly tortured to death in there. Lydia leaned against the sink and closed her eyes. No, it was not Katherine and the man who were embarrassed. Lydia was stuck there, she could have moved, but she couldn't move. Her embarrassment was the most pure and involving emotion she had ever felt. It evaporated the flimsy shield of optimism that had served no function but to keep all the trillion things in the world away from her tiny happiness. Then all of the objects in the bathroom began to evaporate one by one. The man was making noises now too. First the sink Lydia was leaning against evaporated, then the door of the crucial stall. There were his hairy buttocks. Her dress was up around her waist. He still had on his tuxedo jacket. Then the walls of the bathroom evaporated, and the walls of the hotel dining room next door, and all of the guests were milling around, and all of their eyes were fixed not on Katherine and the man, but on Lydia: they all knew something Lydia would never know; they could see Lydia, plain as day, and Lydia would never see what they were seeing. The man with the long blond hair behind the electric organ smiled with his red lips and said, "Everyone back on the dance floor because they're—CLEARING AWAY THE ENTRÉES!" Tall, elegant, streamlined couples danced while staring at Lydia. They were dancing on air. The band was playing the animal howls of Katherine and Rasputin. Blood trickled from the gash on his cheek. There were no more buildings in all of California, just the little people at the wedding in the middle of nowhere. There was no more California—just space, and Lydia was falling, or floating, she was light, she too was evaporating, everyone saw clean through Lydia, and she didn't give a damn.

———

LYDIA LEFT THE BATHROOM. SHE WAS TWENTY-FIVE YEARS OLD. She wondered if her life would get better or worse. Worse. It didn't frighten her.

When dessert was served, Katherine came back to the table and sat and talked with Lydia for a while. Lydia was far away. Then Katherine asked her to dance. Lydia was serene. She let Katherine take her hand and walk her to the dance floor.

"We're so ugly!" Katherine said, positively glowing with pleasure.

"Ugly?" Lydia said. "I'll tell you what's ugly. Right now some Muslim woman in Bosnia is being raped with a bayonet. That's ugly. We're beautiful."

"Lydia, you're drunk!" The girls danced, sometimes holding each other.

In a corner of the hotel dining room, Rasputin and Cal, the best man, drank champagne and gazed out at the two bridesmaids dancing.

Said Cal to his older brother's friend, "What'd you fuck her for? You should've fucked the maid of honor."

Doctor Mom

Over the years, the mothers of America have
had a kind of medical training. . . . And now
at home, the mothers of America are putting
this advice to work.

—TV advertisement for cough medicine

SHE IS A STERN LADY. WHEN HER HUSBAND AND CHILDREN get sick, which they tend to do often and all at once, she marches them one at a time into her examining room to investigate their bodies with her clinical hands and her cold metal instruments. She is gifted and relentlessly trained. Everybody knows how tough medical school is. She powered her way through it. To this day she keeps up the self-education—reads the journals, tries the new techniques. Long ago, all that discipline burnt the frivolity right out of her. Frivolity she perceives as something liquid, and though by trade she knows she is made mostly of water (of which she consumes a pint beaker at every meal) she perceives herself as a dry solid, and so do the people who know her. This summer, with her husband away doing fieldwork in anthropology, and her medical practice having collapsed as a result of several thorny malpractice suits, she will lie down at night on her examination table and listen to certain songs: Blossom Dearie, Claude Debussy.

What could the family of such a lady be like? Pretty normal, actually. They live in New Jersey. Glasses-face academic husband, a lanky, almost hairless, womanly man who jokes with the kids. Two kids, older sister and younger brother, fourteen and ten this summer. The girl will be leaving for overnight camp. There is no question of an adolescent rebellion against her mom—how could she? There's no chink in this lady's armor. The boy behaves with impunity toward his mom, meaning he treats her as if she were a regular mom. He whines, he kisses, cajoles, licks her arm. "Mom, you have no idea what you're talking about. I can't believe you. You're such a jerk. You're so dumb." He wanders over to her while she's beating an egg, flicks her butt with his thumb. She lets him get away with it, while the daughter is speechless, mouth open, cowed. It's such an improbable and unrealistic thing to do to this woman that she thinks her little brother must be a schizophrenic, someone with personalities, walking around in a dreamworld of his own manufacture. The dad finds all of family life profoundly amusing. He notes the improprieties and violations with a connoisseur's relish. Doctor Mom, because she is afraid of her son, loves him most—he's the only one who understands she's dumb. The father and daughter, who work together in the family by working independently— two solo units orbiting the mother-son nucleus—will abandon the woman and boy for the summer, almost as an experiment: let's see what happens if we leave them at one another's mercy.

Doctor Mom, whose name is Ruth, does not like or respect anthropology. She's fully and uncritically invested in the culture of her own consciousness. She's one of these implacable, objectlike adults who acts and acts, whose mind is opaque to family and friends (except the boy, and him only by intuition). She has no idea why she married the guy, Gary, but she knows it's right.

No one in the world but the boy can picture this woman as anything but a gray matriarch with a short, squared-off haircut to go with her square face and square body. Not even Gary. When Ruth and Gary make love, they do it in the dark without thinking. They don't even know who they are when they are touching each other in bed. Everything is squishy surfaces and body noises. It's aggressive, blind fucking that blots out all cerebral activity, and God bless them that it feels so damn good; they fall asleep together afterward, good night and good-bye, and then it's breakfast time and Dad is joking with the kids and Mom is off working somehow on something, even now that she's been banished from her profession. She doesn't care if Gary goes off for months at a time to practice ethnography, whatever that is, or she doesn't think she cares, and in her mind there is no difference between the two, no time for or interest in reflection.

———————

GUIDED BY THE INVISIBLE GOD OF FAMILY COINCIDENCE, GARY
and his daughter, Samantha, have managed to be leaving
home on the same hot day at the end of June; one last
farewell examination by Doctor Mom, because they both
have coughs; so does the boy, Rodney. Ruth never gets sick,
and when she does, nobody knows except her. Illness doesn't
do a thing for her, there's not a bacterium or virus out there
that could lay her low, she can take anything and keep going,
she'd punch an amoeba right in the mitochondria and that
thing would curdle up and die, and she'd step on its head
while marching away in her cushioned white shoes.

She's got the three people in her family lined up on the
hard wooden bench in the anteroom to her home office. It's
not clear whether she's trying to be amusing as she stands
erect in the threshold, festooned with a stethoscope, eyebrows arched, mouth a flat line, tablespoon and cough-syrup
bottle gripped in one hand, bony-strong finger of the other
hand beckoning like the finger of the witch who stood in the
doorway of the gingerbread house. Rodney goes in first.
Today she's peremptory with him—this one she's got all summer to probe and diagnose and treat. She slaps the cold
stethoscope around the delicious unmarked cylinder of his
torso; tongue depressor; "Say 'ah.' "

"Awwwch, Mom, you're gagging me!"

In goes the cough syrup, pat on the butt from Doctor Mom, "Send your sister in," and the boy is done.

Ruth is quick with the girl, too. Samantha gets a kiss on the forehead instead of a pat, and for the first time she feels some sarcasm stirring in her, just below the achy-tacky post–cough-syrup sensation in the back of her throat, but she can't spit it out, not yet; maybe at the end of the summer. For now she's an obedient, nice, friendless, out-of-it teenager, the only fourteen-year-old in America who doesn't know what sarcasm is—what is that thing under her throat? Ick, she wants a glass of water.

And then comes Gary, with bedroom eyes. Ruth meets him with examination-room eyes. Gary looks at his feet dejectedly, and that's when a couple of tears escape down Ruth's face. She has a mental image of her and Gary sitting side by side on the examining table, fingers entwined, legs dangling over the edge, swaying gently back and forth as if they were on a Ferris wheel. She lets it go. It would be against everything she stands for not to examine Gary swiftly and skillfully and send him on his way as she did her children, though he will not be going to summer baseball clinic for the day, as her son will be, nor to overnight camp in the Adirondacks for the summer, as her daughter will be, but to northern Africa, until November, to mingle with the peoples. They call them "peoples" instead of "people." She can relate to that, but "informants" is a funny word. And then her man and her girl are gone.

Rodney will maintain his cough all summer long. Though Mom rules out bronchitis almost right off the bat, and tuberculosis not long after, the cough will hover nonetheless like a sweet and heavy perfume about his summer's bouquet of florid symptomatology.

———————

ON THE FIRST DAY AFTER HE AND HIS MOTHER HAVE BEEN LEFT alone, Rodney turns the upstairs hallway into a sports complex. He's got bats and balls up there, and he's wearing a striped baseball uniform and a jockstrap and, just for the hell of it, a groin cup. Doctor Mom, despite the suspension of her license, is downstairs treating the occasional loyal and surreptitious patient for next to nothing, and doing God knows what else in there, while upstairs Rodney has lined the bare oak floor of the hallway with foam-rubber exercise mats to practice his slide into home plate. He works up speed for half the length of the hallway, descends onto his hip and thigh, skims the surface of the hallway on his gym mats as if on a magic carpet, and *pow!* into the closed door of his sister's room at the end of the hall. One time he doesn't notice the gap that has opened up between two of the gym mats, lands precisely in the gap, slides directly along the floor itself, and gets a big jagged oak splinter in his ass. It's not really in his ass, it's in his upper thigh, but he thinks of it as his ass, and when he opens the door of the examining room where his mother is in mid-mammogram with a voluptuous thirty-year-old patient, he says, "Doctor Mom, I got a splinter in my ass."

"In the waiting room, now!"

A few moments after the lady walks by him clutching the collar of her shirt, Ruth calls him in sternly. "Take off your pants and lie on the table."

He's lying there on his side, his little naked hip exposed. She has on her reading glasses that look like the lower half of a pair of normal glasses. She swabs the area of the wound with alcohol. The sensation of wet coolness on his thigh is the bliss he feels when his mother pays attention to him. He cries a little now. She observes the jockstrap-and-cup arrangement, and it amuses her. Most of the splinter comes out with a tweezer, but it's a splintery splinter so she needs to pierce the surface of the skin with a sterilized pin for the small particles. This gives him an opportunity to cry a little more.

That night, two hours after Rodney has gone to bed, Ruth is climbing the stairs in her white terrycloth bathrobe when she hears him call out to her. She enters the dark room. "My hip is really sore from today. I think I bruised it. I can't sleep."

She goes down to her office, retrieves an ice pack, carries it up. The lights are on in Rod's room, and he's lying naked on top of the covers. She applies the pack to the bone bruise of her boy. "Hold that there for a second," she says. She walks to the wall, shuts off the light, comes back, sits on the edge of the bed and takes over holding the ice pack there in silence for a while.

"Do you miss them?" he asks.

"Yes," she says with a neutral expression on her face in the dark room.

"I miss them," he says. "How much do you miss them?"

"Lot."

"What would happen if they died?"

"They won't."

"What would happen?"

"What do you mean what would happen?"

"If they died, would you die?"

"No."

"I never thought about it before, but I think I might die if they died."

"I will not let you die."

"What if they died *and* I died? Then would you die? Like let's say Sammy falls off a cliff—and okay, she doesn't die right away, she lies there at the bottom of the cliff for ten hours of excruciating agony and the whole time the rescue team is trying to get to her and then she dies in agony. And a couple of days later Dad gets caught in a holy war and he's taken hostage by terrorists and the Americans won't meet the terrorists' demands so they cut off Dad's head and they send the Americans a videotape of Dad with his head cut off and then the media gets ahold of the tape and they put a picture of Dad's bloody stump neck on the front page of the newspaper. So far, would you die?"

"Nope."

"Okay, so then, what if I'm walking by a newspaper and I see the picture of Dad's neck even though you tried to keep all newspapers away from me and then all of my molecules, like, speed up all at once, and don't tell me it couldn't happen because I asked my science teacher and he said it's very rare but it does happen, and my molecules all go fast at once and *fhhhht!* I explode in the bathtub. Then would you die?"

"No."

"You're so tough, Mom," he says, rolling his eyes. "You're a god to me."

"Good night, Rod." This is one of the rare instances when she has spoken his name. It's not quite an endearment, but it's something. Mom doesn't listen to Blossom Dearie tonight. She goes to bed in her bathrobe feeling dizzy.

FIRST LETTERS FROM SAMANTHA AND GARY ARRIVE ON THE SAME day two weeks after the splinter, which means that Gary, who is in Morocco, wrote almost as soon as his nonstop flight from Kennedy touched down in Marrakesh, while Samantha, who is three hundred miles north in the Adirondacks, waited a week and a half before putting pen to paper for Mom and Rod.

Gary's letter is amused and anecdotal. His daily exchanges with other humans—flight attendants, for example—bear the stamp of his profession, which he loves and wants to share with his family. But he knows the folks back home don't get it, his kid because he's too young and his wife because she's not built that way. There is a longing in this letter that all the geographical distance gives him an excuse to express.

Samantha's letter to her mother and brother is a how-are-you-I-am-fine letter. "We played soccer and softball. The food is good. I like my counselors. Please send an extra sweater. Love you Mom. Hi Rod." The letter she wrote to her father on the third day of camp is more revealing: "Dear Dad, I think I'm liking camp pretty well but it's hard to tell. Dad, how can you tell if you're enjoying your own life? What are you supposed to do to make sure your life is good? Also, what is life? Please write back soon. Love, Sammy."

After Rodney has read the letters to his mother, she says, "How is your pain today?"

"Still there." They are speaking of a dull ache in Rodney's left testicle that turns to exquisite tenderness after baseball practice and then, at night when he is lying in bed, throbs. It's the location that has the boy up in arms. Doctor Mom is calm. She diagnosed epididymitis and put him on antibiotics, but that was a week ago, and since the pain has not diminished, she now schedules him for a postprandial sonogram.

In the examination room she removes his trousers, greases him down, slaps on some latex gloves with, it seems to Rodney, an exaggerated smacking of rubber against flesh. Then the cold electronic pencil mushing softly against his scrotum. Without a nurse, Mom is working both the pencil and the keyboard aspects of the sonogrammatical apparatus. And then they appear on the computer screen—his enormous, white and black, rotogravure balls, discrete and complicated organisms, intelligent life from outer space, astral, televised, filled with mystery. "Varicocele, i.e., enlarged blood vessel. I should have guessed. I mean known. Nothing serious. Thought to inhibit fertility, but that's not a concern for us. Elective surgery is indicated."

"Elective surgery. What's that mean?"

"That means it's not emergency surgery."

"Does it mean I get to decide if I have it or not?"

"No. Let's just do it now and get it over with."

"I don't really feel so good. I just ate milk and cookies, and you're not supposed to eat before elective surgery."

"That's only for general anesthesia. You'll be having local."

"I think you're wrong on this one, Mom. I think it's all surgery. Let's look it up."

"Shush, Rodney."

"I'm not having the surgery."

"Are you questioning my medical judgment?" She's raised her voice now. She's looming above him in her white coat with those big eyebrows like a gigantic science fiction robot mom who has taken over all political control in the final days of human life on the planet. Lying supine on the cool vinyl table, pants around his ankles, groin-deep in diagnostic equipment, Rodney is not exactly in a position of power. "Take this." She gives him a pill with water. "Stay there." She extricates his pants and underpants from his ankles and carries the pants-enshrouded undies from the room.

Lying there, Rodney hatches a scheme to run away from home. He'll take off down the street just like that—bottom-less—away from the horror of Doctor Mom. Man, does he feel good about this plan all over his body. He gets up and runs for the door and falls flat on his face. "That would be the muscle relaxant taking effect," says Ruth, walking through the door, scrubbed and wearing surgical greens. She hauls him back onto the table.

"Make a fist and relax. Make a fist and relax. Make a fist and relax." At no point does she give him a thorough briefing on the surgery, which is too bad because he thinks she's going to cut his balls per se. She will not: the incision is placed northeast of the actual crotch. She slips a needle into the back of his hand and fills it with a sedative. "You'll be conscious during surgery, but you won't remember it. You'll feel a few pricks as I apply the local."

Rod is trying to form a dirty joke about feeling a prick, but he can't say it out loud because that lady is his mother. Right now words are somewhere deep inside his body, far away from the place where his mouth meets the world. He likes the feeling of thinking way back down inside his body— it's got to be the drugs that are making that happen. He'll give up baseball, he thinks, and devote his adolescence to drug abuse.

Mom says, "What I'm doing here with the needles is blocking the nerves in the region." She places a screen over his belly so he won't see what's going on down below. He sees her shoulders moving to make him think she's now cutting his body, which she is.

There he is beneath her, the whole biological boy, inside and outside. If she were a different woman—if she were a man, for that matter, she thinks—the feeling she has now while clamping this blood vessel of her open son would make her legs shake, would make her weep, not in distress or horror, but in the presence of unspeakable beauty.

"What are the drugs that make you choke on your own vomit?" he asks dreamily, while his mom works on his body.

"I won't let you choke."

"What do you think Dad's doing right now?"

"Mingling with indigenous peoples."

"What about Sammy?"

"Eating a burnt marshmallow."

"I miss them, Mom. Do you miss them?"

"Don't talk to your mother while she's ligating your spermatic vein."

"Can I just ask one more thing?"

"What?"

"Can I just ask three more things?"

"One."

"Do you love me?"

"Yes."

"Do you love Dad?"

"Shush."

"You don't love Dad?"

"If I hear one more question, young man, it's general anesthesia for you."

———

FIVE DAYS POST-OP, A LETTER ARRIVES FROM SAMANTHA. RUTH had called her an hour after surgery to let her know it was a success. She had wanted to call Gary, but he was in the Sahara. When Ruth has pictured Gary in the Sahara, she has pictured him *in* the Sahara, lying down in the sand, covered up by the sand, turning into sand, becoming a sand dune. She can feel the sand on her skin, taste the sand in her mouth. This natural capacity to hold a human body inside her own body is the gift that makes her a superb diagnostician, but this sand business jars her unquestioned sense of herself as roving instrument of empirical knowledge.

" 'Dear Mom and Rod,' " Ruth reads aloud from Samantha's prescient letter at the kitchen table, " 'Summer camp is nice. I climbed a mountain today. Saw a bear. Drank water from a stream. Got stung by an ant. I am glad to hear the surgery went well. I like my counselors and the other kids. Maybe next Rod will have a sports injury in his knee. Mom, you can plant a steel rod in his knee. Then he will really be Rod-knee. Get it? Love to Mom. Hi to Rod. Samantha.' "

Quietly Rod asks, "Do you think Sammy doesn't love me?" Mom doesn't answer. They're both stunned by this letter from a girl who has been demure and submissive to them all her life. Now this baldfaced cheek and depraved indifference to the intactness of the boy's body. The two homebodies are morose for the rest of the evening. "Why aren't we far away, Mom? How come they're the ones who get to be far away?"

"Rodney, I think you should go back to baseball clinic tomorrow."

"No, Mom. The operation." He's whining. It's not like him to wimp out on baseball.

"I'll wake you at seven."

"But my wounds are still healing."

"Wound."

"What?"

"One incision. One wound."

"What?"

"One incision!"

"But my wounds are still healing."

———————

ON THE DAY THAT HER JOKEY LETTER JOSTLES THE FOLKS BACK home, Samantha receives a letter from her dad in reply to the yearning, philosophical letter she sent him. "Dear Samantha, Your letter moved me. It has been several days since I first read it, and I have read it many times and thought about it. Even as I write these words I'm wondering how to respond. The sky is so steep and tall here in the desert. It gets very cold at night and the moon is brighter than anywhere else in the world. People are friendlier here at night than they are during the day. At night they invite you into their homes and sprinkle water on your head and their children's heads. In the day it feels like all they do is haggle. The moon is exquisite. I can't wait for night to come so I can look at the moon. It's everything you want a moon to be. When I look at the moon I am filled with joy and sadness because I know it is the same moon you are looking at, maybe right now through the window of your cabin in the Adirondacks. I think this is my attempt to answer your questions. How'm I doing? Love, Dad."

———————

TEN DAYS HAVE PASSED SINCE THE VARICOCELE. THE MARK OF surgery is no longer more than another abrasion on the surface of an active, sports-minded boy, but Rodney has begun having a little bit of hearing loss and a few other problems physically coping with reality. The Doctor Mom radar has picked up on these, plus a new crankiness and cowed, needy quality in someone who is normally able to dominate her by sheer confidence. She conducts a casual line of inquiry at the kitchen table during dinner.

"How's baseball?"

"Fine. Okay."

"Just okay?"

"No, it's good, it's great." Rod is sullen.

"You're not eating."

"I'm not hungry."

"What's the matter at baseball?"

"Nothing."

"Rodney."

"I'm not finding the sweet spot. I'm not connecting with the ball. I'm missing the ball. I'm striking out."

"A slump?"

"A slump."

"What does it feel like when you can't hit the ball?"

"Like my arms won't move right."

"Dizziness?"

"Yeah."

"Vertigo?"

"What's vertigo?"

"Dizziness."

"Yeah."

"Hearing loss?"

"I don't know."

"Headaches?"

"First thing in the morning."

"Ringing?"

"In my left ear."

"You've been sighing a lot."

"I'm bummed."

"What are you bummed about?"

"Being bummed."

After dinner, in the examination room, Ruth asks Rodney where his fingers are. Where are they now? Where are they now? Where are they now? With a pointy flashlight, she looks through his ear hole into the darkness of his inner head. She has him walk a line. She taps him on the chin with a hammer and watches his face twitch. These tests feel silly to Rod, but

Mom is handy here, she's good with her hands. What's more, she's resourceful. "Go read a book," she says, and hustles down to the basement, where she concocts a something with Gary's woodworking equipment and some loose electronic gadgetry that happens to be lying around. It's a pair of goggles connected to electromagnets with tiny pistons that pierce the surface of the goggle and point inward toward the eyelids of the wearer. She calls Rodney back from the book he was not reading, places the goggles on his head, and stretches him out on the examination table, site of much low-level household biological drama. She attaches the goggles to a precision timing device and juices up the electromagnets. At regular intervals, the pistons poke Rodney oh-so-lightly in the eyelids, and she records the delay in the facial reflexes they evoke. Grimly, she sends him off to bed.

Lying on the same table in the dark after Rodney is asleep, Ruth mouths the words "Give him the ooh-la-la" along with Blossom Dearie. She gets up and turns off the CD, which is not producing the desired effect. She doesn't know what effect she desires, she just knows that statistically a few Dearie renditions have been known to produce it. She stands for a while on the threshold of the examination room in comfortable stretch slacks and a loose pullover. She really needs to do a CT scan of Rod, a tomography of the petrous bone, and three to four skull films. She doesn't own some of the equipment, but she won't let anybody else do these tests.

She must do them herself. That's how fiercely she loves her son.

At just the moment when Ruth is agreeing over the phone to blow the family nest egg on a cut-rate CT scanner she will obtain illegally from a guy, her daughter, Samantha, is composing a letter to Gary in Africa by the light of an Adirondack moon. "Dear Dad, you are such a good dad! I think I want to become a poet. When I'm a poet and people are interviewing me on the radio about my latest poem, I will tell them that my dad used to write me beautiful letters about the moon and other things when he was in the Sahara Desert, and that's why I became a poet. Do you think Mom is a good mom? I think Mom is a good doctor and maybe you can't be a good doctor and a good mom at the same time. I feel different than I've ever felt before. I love you Daddy. XO Sammy."

———

SEVERAL WEEKS LATER, AT BREAKFAST ON THE MORNING AFTER THE radical, home-administered brain tests, Mom gives Rod a pill. "What's this?"

"Prednisone."

"What's it for?"

"Darling, you have what's called an acoustic neuroma. I'm going to have to operate, and the prednisone will prepare your body for the operation."

"Don't call me darling."

"An acoustic neuroma is a progressively enlarging benign tumor of the eighth cranial nerve. It's the nerve that has to do with hearing."

"I have a brain tumor?"

"It's benign."

"I don't have a brain tumor!" Rodney grasps an uncooked egg from the carton on the kitchen counter. "This is my brain. This is my brain with an acoustic neuroma." He crushes the egg in his hand. Soft yolk and white burst out in every direction. He picks up another egg. "Watch. Brain. Neuroma." He mashes this one against the table. Ruth gets splattered.

"Wash your hand and take your pill and clean up this mess."

"No."

Ruth stands up, grabs Rodney by the elbow, drags him to the sink, and turns on the spigot. She holds his egg hand under the water, soaps it, and abrades it harshly and unpleasantly. He is wailing and struggling, but she is much stronger than he is. This is like a little three-year-old having a tantrum, and his mother assumes the businesslike demeanor of moms the world over who know how to handle unruly toddlers. It's hard to know what the demeanor conceals in such women. That's the point. She shoves the steroid down his throat and sends him off to baseball clinic.

When she is tucking him in that night they are both in softer moods. Each respects the other for the admirable struggle of that morning. They let their hair down a little and make their own special version of mom-and-son talk. Rod doesn't exactly want to die, but he wouldn't mind dying. He sort of does want to die. He thinks of dying as something cool to do that no one else his age is doing, really. Death might be like going to Morocco. "Would you still love me if I was dead?" he asks.

"Yes."

"More than you do now?"

"No."

"Less than you do now?"

"Same."

"I think if I die you'll *feel* like you love me more, even if you really don't."

"I'd be much sadder."

"What do you mean, much sadder? You mean you're sad now?"

"No, I didn't mean that."

"Why did you say much sadder?"

"Forget it."

"Maybe with my new brain tumor I'll forget it."

"Ha ha."

"What's it like to die?"

"Nothing."

"It has to be like something."

"No, I don't think it's like anything." As she is saying this, Ruth senses what it will be like. Everything will be resolved into its purest form. There will be sixteen colors, each clearly distinguishable from the others. All corporeal things will assume the shapes intelligible to Euclidean geometry: rectangles, circles, spheres, cubes, cylinders. All noises will be music, all thoughts discrete. In death there will be no ambiguity. She is appalled at herself for thinking such things because she knows death is nothing. Over the course of the summer, Ruth has found herself in the thrall of these increasingly long reveries. They are torture. Where are her husband and daughter when she needs them?

As if in answer to that question, there is a letter from Gary awaiting Ruth in the vestibule, overlooked by her and Rodney in the day's nerve hullabaloo. By now she can't lie still and listen to music anymore. Music has proved frivolous as she always knew it would. She has taken to wandering the house at night instead of sleeping, and on her fourth or fifth excursion through the vestibule, she spots the envelope that contains Gary's unhappy letter.

"Dear Ruth, There has been a setback in the research. An Algerian attack on the border killed ten people in the community I've been working with. Population tends to increase at a faster rate than its means of subsistence, and unless it is checked by moral restraint or by disease, famine, war, or other disaster, widespread poverty and degradation inevitably result. I was planning to stay here until the end of November but I can't face it. I'll be back on the Friday of Labor Day weekend." It was after Gary received the poet letter from Samantha that he composed this letter to Ruth. Sammy's letter depressed Gary so. He did not mean to encourage misogyny in his daughter. Did he?

Ruth is satisfied with Gary's letter. She makes a beeline for her CD of Claude Debussy's *Images* for one more try. Sure enough, lying there in the dark, she can visualize the chords coming toward her; she sees them slicing the air into mathematically precise flaps, as a surgeon's scalpel would do to flesh. All is well.

———

TUMOR REMOVAL HAPPENS ON A SWELTERING DAY AT THE BEGINning of the second week of August, but neither mother nor son feels the heat. The house is locked down, sealed off, and holding steady at seventy degrees Fahrenheit. In fact, there are two areas in the world. One of them is the area outside the house, the other is the area inside the house.

Ruth enters Rodney's room at six A.M. with thirty-two milligrams of prednisone. She's looking crisp and virile and alert, and her short grayish brown hair is especially squared off today, all of which comforts Rodney.

Over the last few days, Ruth has been down in Gary's basement workshop building a home version of the Mayfield-Kees skeletal fixation headrest, which will immobilize the patient's head completely and comfortably. At seven-fifteen A.M., as he's sliding drowsily into the apparatus, Rodney notices that the actual head clamp itself is merely Dad's extra-large woodworking vise grip with tiny soft pillows glued on, and he has a final tantrum before his mother enters his brain.

The anesthesiology for this procedure is more complicated than any she remembers from her surgical rotation, but she's propped open the relevant issue of *Benign Tumor Monthly,* where there is a step-by-step guide to the whole thing. Throughout surgery, she consults it as a reasonably experienced chef might consult a recipe book during the preparation of a new dish.

She starts to panic. This is after she has made the cuts in the patient's scalp, made burr holes in his skull, and removed a small, circular chunk of suboccipital bone. Because what if there isn't really a tumor? What if she imagined it? She's pretty sure she saw a darkened rounded area on the CT scan, and yes, this teeny-tiny thing in Rodney's exposed eighth cranial nerve sure doesn't *seem* like it belongs there, but on the other hand Ruth doesn't have a whole lot of experience looking at actual cranial nerves and maybe they're just bumpy, maybe they all naturally come with nondangerous bumps like that, but sometimes you gotta go on faith with these types of things, and she gets the damn bump out of there and tosses it in the garbage and closes him up by grafting a little skin from another part of his head over the wound, and he's going to be okay, they both made it through this bloody operation and they're both alive and Gary and Samantha will be home in a couple of weeks and then everything can get back to normal, if only the state of New Jersey would give her back her medical license.

THE BIG SURPRISE AND MOST HARROWING CLINICAL EVENT OF THE summer comes on the Friday before Labor Day. Gary is sitting on an Air France 747 over the Atlantic Ocean observing the ritually inflected speech patterns of flight attendants, and the most beautiful seventeen-year-old counselor is letting Samantha lightly touch his penis in the bathroom of the chartered Adirondack Trailways camp bus as it hurtles southward on Route 87, while back at home Doctor Mom is in Rodney's bedroom standing over Rodney, who has just vomited on her white shoes. She prods his abdomen and softly whispers these words: "Nausea, anorexia, rapid pulse rate, diffuse tenderness, no abdominal distension, hyperesthesia of the

skin near McBurney's point, localized rebound tenderness";
his mother's words, like the saddest song he has ever heard,
make Rodney cry. "You've got acute appendicitis, kiddo."

"Don't call me kiddo."

This is an operation Ruth performed a zillion times
asleep on her feet in her residency. Hell, she's tempted to
open him up in his bedroom and hack that thing out of there
with a sharp pocketknife, but Ruth is nothing if not a stickler
for protocol, so she brings him down to what has become the
surgical theater, aggressively replenishes his fluids, knocks
him out with sodium pentathol, and performs the emergency
appendectomy.

This time when she is inside her only boy-o, something
awful happens inside of Ruth. She weeps—first open weeping in years. Her legs are shaking. It's all she can do to clamp
that ridiculous vestigial sac, place the ligature, suture up,
and get out of her son.

She's stirred up inside. She can't control her thoughts
and feelings. She remains this way for hours. Maybe from now
on this is how she'll be—Mrs. Mess, unfit to doctor or
mother. She sits with Rodney, holding his little bluish hand,
weeping softly as he emerges from chemical sleep. This is the
position in which Gary and Samantha find them when they
return home from their travels and walk through the door of
the examination room at exactly six P.M. on the Friday of

Labor Day weekend. The last piece of medical news Ruth gave to either of them was the varicocele, and so they're kind of stunned when they see this woman poised over this supine child as in *The Consolation of Philosophy*, weeping, and this groggy boy with a bandage on his head and a fresh wound in his side, moaning. Ruth leaps upon Gary and practically knocks him over. "I blew the nest egg!" she cries.

"What?"

She begins to pour out the summer's entire case history, but Gary stops her. "Let's leave the boy to rest." Gary guides his wife and daughter out of the examination room, which is his wife's domain, and into the living room, which is his domain because he's an anthropologist. Neither of the women in his family wants to go into the living room. Ruth clings to him in the vestibule with all her force and weight. Samantha's got a lot of other things on her mind, wants no tedious family hassle, heads up the stairs to her bedroom. But something stops her at the top of the stairs. Father's girl that she is, what she suddenly becomes interested in here are the relative positions and attitudes of the bodies of her parents. She looks down from the head of the stairs and sees her little mother down in the vestibule so small in her father's arms. Her mother and her father both look so much smaller than, for example, several of the mountains she climbed this summer in the High Peaks region of the Adirondacks.

"I don't know what I'm going to do now, but you'll have to take care of me as I feel my way," Ruth says, wrapped in Gary's arms. "Please don't ever go on a trip without me again."

Gary comforts her as she cries, and he can't help not being able to believe his good fortune that this is the new wife he's come home to. Even as he is distressed to see his wife in such a terrible upset, he can't help wanting to leave again right away for another long trip, with the hope that she'll be even weaker and more submissive next time he comes back; he wouldn't mind a submissive wife for once in his life.

Here comes Rodney into the vestibule, drawn inexorably to tedious family hassle. He's walking an inch at a time with a fair amount of pain. The summer has literally diminished him. He's minus a lump in his head, an appendix, part of a spermatic vein and its collaterals. He's all cut up and scarred, dragging a bag of glucose from his arm.

From the top of the stairs, Samantha calls, "Come here, Tumor Boy, I'll take care of you." Now Rodney is like a whore who loves his work—he'll let just anyone succor him.

He begins the slow, painful journey up the stairs to his sister. Samantha stands on high gazing down at her brother, toward whom her intentions are only the best. She will take care of him now—she's got the power. She sees her mother's shoulders shaking with grief, and each undulation of that exhausted, sobbing body is like a jolt of electrical energy through Samantha's limbs and brain. For the first time in her life she's thinking clearly, she knows who she is, she knows what she wants. "Come on, Rod. That's my little bundle of infection, only three steps to go." Rodney is faint with pain, but he's so happy that his sister has grown several inches over the summer, that she's finally acting the way an older sister should.

Someone left the front door open. The house is getting warm and steamy. The neighbors are having a barbecue. All at once, the pungent odor of searing meat hits the olfactory organs of the four people in this family on another Friday night toward the end of summer in the suburbs of northern New Jersey.

A Bird Accident

Only one had the power of a "Bird" called
Parker. . . . Only one plays like this. . . .
The great performers are always creating a
higher standard.

—*TV advertisement for a car*

SOMEONE IS RUNNING OVER CHARLIE PARKER WITH A Cadillac. Even as he's being run over, Parker is playing the plastic alto saxophone that he used in the famous Massey Hall concert in Toronto after hocking his real, metal saxophone to buy heroin. On a country road, the Cadillac is running over his foot, and Parker is playing "The Man I Love" on his plastic sax. As he is playing it, he changes the lyrics to "The Man I Love," even though he's playing it and not singing it. The new lyrics are, "Someday he'll come along, the man I love, and he'll be a big and strong advertising executive and he'll run over my foot with a Cadillac." When you hear the way Charlie "Bird" Parker is playing that song, you feel two things: you feel the heroin spreading out like music in your body, and you feel a big heavy Cadillac creeping up your leg. The Cadillac is up to your ankle now, because it's up to his ankle and up to the ankle of the song. The luxury sedan is breaking the shin of the song. This would sound a bit like free jazz: attentive, pained. You can't even feel this kind of pain it's so painful. All you can do is soldier on through it. It helps if you've got an alto saxophone and you're brave enough to make music that rivals the angels' music in heaven. In heaven there is no pain involved in making music. It's harder for the angels to make water than it is for them to make music, because they have no bodies. Parker has a big corpulent bird body, and his knees are being crushed. His thighs are being crushed, his dick and his balls are being crushed—parts of his body getting to know one another for the first time—his hips are being crushed. Once again he's making music the hard way.

He's still playing "The Man I Love," but he's mixing in changes from "Lover Man." People have remarked how agile Parker is when he's inside one song and he reaches out, takes hold of a second song and draws it into the first. People have said, "How effortless, how pretty," but now the joining of these two songs, "The Man I Love" and "Lover Man," sounds like two solid objects trying to occupy the same space at the same time—a man and a car, for example. And what you hear in the music is that the car is winning, physically, while the man is winning, morally. Moral victory doesn't make easy listening. Charlie Parker's ribs are shattered to pieces by the big metal Cadillac, and his clavicle cracks, and his windpipe is flattened like an empty tube of toothpaste squeezed from the bottom. His chin is crushed next, and the embouchure that changed the sound of music forever. Then his brain is made into a chunky red oatmeal by the car. Nevertheless, he is able to squeeze thirty-two more notes into the final measure of "The Man I Love."

Meanwhile, the driver of the car has had the automatic window down and he's been listening to the song. He's a white ad exec with mixed feelings about what he's doing. He didn't really think this thing through before he did it. Not that it would have required much thought: you're going fifty in a Cadillac, and you hit someone. It's a basic traditional concept in advertising, to combine the name of your product with the name of a famous person everyone likes. This guy thought, why not take it a step further, combine the actual car with the actual guy. He's okay, really, the ad man; let's call him Saatchi&Saatchi Worldwide (that's not his real name, nor should he in any way be associated with the venerable international agency which also bears that name). He has a family and wants to do the right thing for them. He figures, I'll do a good turn for Cadillac, Cadillac will be happy, I'll get a bonus to sock away for my kid's education, plus I'll be doing something creative, which will help to relieve the stresses and tensions that build up inside a guy working in such a competitive field.

Charlie Parker is lying in the mud doing soft arpeggios. Saatchi&Saatchi is not unmoved by this. He steps out of his car and stands above Parker. Parker looks up at him, asks a question: "What's the most important national holiday for the American Negro?"

"I don't know, Martin Luther King Day?"

"Nope. March tenth."

"March tenth? What's March tenth?"

"The day the Cadillacs come off the assembly line." (This is Parker's famous irrepressible wit.)

"Can I get you to a hospital?"

"What would be the point?"

"Well, is there anything I can do for you?"

"Run me over again," says the wet, mangled corpse.

Saatchi&Saatchi shrugs. "Okay."

When a bone breaks under pressure, the fat that is stored inside the bone may shoot out into the bloodstream. A big clump of congealed fat may wander the blood vessels and come to rest in the brain, where it may then kill a man, or put him in a coma. That's what happens to Bird, the second time the guy runs him over. It's a well-known fact among jazz people that the up-tempo numbers are easier to play than the ballads, and what with a wad of fat lodged in his brain now, Parker decides to play "Celerity."

Saatchi&Saatchi really is a jazz fan, though he prefers the contemporary jazz sound that calms your nerves instead of agitating them when you're in a rush-hour traffic jam halfway out to the country. Still, being a jazz fan, he is happy to involve himself with a giant like Parker, if only to run him over with his car. Bird is not happy, but he has this terrible event to fight against, which is what he has always needed to make his strange, almost careless noises. Even now, he is doing what he does best—musically documenting his own oppression and death. As the Cadillac breaks his body, so he is able to break time. He breaks open a second and fills it with a lot of littler seconds, each one seeming to take forever to happen, just as this car accident feels to him as if it has always happened and will always happen. It's beautiful that Bird can do this, and Bird is someone who shows with commanding authority what ugliness beauty must bear.

Other people notice the accident on the country road; other ad men, mostly. Their first response: *I want to run over a great musician, too.* They are envious of the niche Saatchi&Saatchi has cleared out for himself by running over Parker in particular. Sometimes the guy who comes up with the idea doesn't quite get it right, and another guy can step in and nail the idea, but in this case, Charlie Parker is the perfect person to run over, and the Cadillac is the perfect car to run him over with. The other ad men are thinking of hitting Armstrong and Ellington and Tatum and Gillespie and Davis with their cars. It won't have the same oomph as hitting Parker with a Cadillac, but in advertising second-best counts for a lot, so now these other fellows climb into their respective luxury sedans and start running over genius musicians, out on a country road. Duke Ellington gets his hands crushed into the keys of the piano by a sleek Lexus. Ellington howls, and it sounds as if he's counting off some insane Lindy for coked-out dancers on slapstick celluloid. Dizzy Gillespie's patented enormous trumpet cheeks, when flattened by the radial tires of an Acura Legend, spread out over miles of American terrain.

The cars are ten abreast now, as are the advertising executives behind the wheels and the musicians beneath them. On that country road, many of the revolutionaries of American music in the twentieth century have come together in a single bloody ensemble. It's a sad day for music. It's not such a great day for advertising, either.

Miles Davis, when hit, scowls, remains compact and unified in his dark little body, and refuses to play a single note.

Acknowledgments

Many thanks to Paul Allman, Michelle Araujo, Nick Balaban, Mike Ballou, Jeanne Marie Beaumont, Adrienne Brodeur, Gabriel Brownstein, E. Shaskan Bumas, Ken Foster, Sam Greenhoe, Jennifer Hengen, Anna Borst Henry, Michael Henry, Rita Jackevicius, Roland Kelts, Nora Krug, Joel Lovell, Brian McLendon, Martha McPhee, Betsey Mills, Virginia Picchi, Carol Plum, Sara Powers, Anna Rabinowitz, Allen Ross, Sergio Santos, Lore Segal, Carole Sharpe, Myron Sharpe, Adam Simon, Jefferey Simons, Jacqueline Steiner, Robert "Bob" Sullivan, Suzanne Sullivan, Bruce Tracy, Eliza Truitt, and Joel Weinstein.

About the Author

MATTHEW SHARPE has published stories in *Harper's, Zoetrope, Southwest Review, Mississippi Mud,* and *American Letters & Commentary.* He lives in New York.